THE INTERN INSTALLMENT COMPLETE SERIES

AN ALPHA BILLIONAIRE ROMANCE

MICHELLE LOVE

CONTENTS

Made in "The United States" by:

Michelle Love

© Copyright 2021

ISBN: 978-1-64808-369-3

❀ Created with Vellum

BLURB

Damon

I ran one of the most successful architecture companies in the world, well-known to everyone in the business. I was involved in every aspect of the daily activities, though one of my least favorite parts was interviewing for interns every year.

It was something that came along with the company. and it was a great learning tool for the students, so I kept the policy. I just typically left it to my managers, who were more hands-on with the teams, to decide who to hire out of all of the faces that we saw.

I started caring more, however, the moment that Elisa walked in the door. She was everything that I didn't look for in a woman: sweetness, innocence, and inexperience. She was guarded and intelligent, and I fought to keep her out of my company, against the wishes of everyone else at that interview.

Elisa

I was excited about the interview to intern at Elkus Manfredi Architecture, since it carved out a perfect future for me. I excelled at school and was recommended for the position, a condition that wasn't easy to fulfill. I dressed the part, made the perfect resume outlining my experience, and went into the building with my head high.

Then I saw the most gorgeous man that I'd ever seen in my life. He first caught my attention in the elevator and then in the room where I was to be interviewed.

I knew that, regardless of whether I got the position or not, I'd never forget the way that he had made me feel. I'd never forget the way he heated me up and shook me to my very core.

Could I handle working with him? Could I ignore the intensity between us with my future in mind?

1

THE INTERN INSTALLMENT BOOK 1

An Alpha Billionaire Romance

By Michelle Love

2

DAMON

It was dark and cold outside as I left my building for my morning run, nodding as the doorman told me to be careful. I loved fall in Boston and preferred it to the crowds that jogged in the summer, getting in my way and throwing off my day. I started to jog at an even pace and headed towards the crosswalk to go over to the Boston Common Park as I looked around at the empty streets, apart from cabs and early morning commuters. This was when I liked the city—when I could focus.

It was still dark outside, and I took deep breaths of the chilled air and started through the trail that made its way through the center of the park. Everything was in shades of fall now; the leaves, yellow, orange and red as they drifted down to the ground in the early morning. It made it worthwhile to avoid this place later in the day, when everyone would gather with their cameras of various kinds and go on about the foliage.

Yes, it was pretty enough, and I appreciated fall. I just didn't see the need to keep talking about it. I wanted quiet and peace. I wanted to think about my day and prepare my mind for the hour-long workout that I'd be doing after this five-mile run. It was a ritual of mine, followed by a long, thorough shower before I dressed for work.

I was the CEO of one of the most successful architecture companies in the world, Elkus Manfredi. The company was established fifty
years ago, and had several locations in some of the bigger American
cities and even in a few other countries. I could work wherever I
chose to, though I preferred to stay in Boston. I knew the city and
could find my way here without a lot of fuss, though I traveled when
needed for the company. It was a welcome break from my day-to-day
routine, and I enjoyed seeing what was happening in the company,
feeling great pride over the growth I'd seen in the last six years.

Home was home, though.

I ran past the pond, where the ground was covered with leaves
and the wind blew around me. I was dressed in my new jogging
clothes, light enough to run in, but warm enough to keep me
comfortable. I jogged steadily as I let my mind move ahead to what
my day entailed.

Every fall, we hired interns from some of the top schools in the
area, depending on our current needs. This year, we would hire two
to help with the teams that planned our buildings, some of which
were world famous. Working with interns wasn't something that I
dealt with personally, apart from being involved in the panel interview. I wanted to make sure that they were a good fit for the company,
given that most of them were close to graduating, and we did
consider hiring them after graduation. I just didn't have any part of
the training and, therefore, took on a lot of responsibilities myself.

I learned about hard work from my father. He ran a construction
company, until he passed away from a heart attack when I was eleven
years old. In the summers, I went into work with him, learning everything that I could. Being from a family of wealth didn't make me lazy,
and I wanted to be the one running a successful company.

My father had nothing to do with my current job, though he'd set
aside a generous trust fund for me before his death, as well as seeing
that Mom was well taken care of. Apparently, at eleven, I could not
take over his company, so his brother did and ruined it within three
years. I always vowed to be better than that.

My job had belonged to my stepfather of five years before he decided to travel with Mom at the ripe old age of fifty-three. Mom was five years younger than he was, and they were in great health to go all over the world on their adventures.

I ran by the statue and toward the other side of town as I thought back to those first days. Some men were capable of taking over the company, men that had a lot of years invested as well as the talent. Kenneth saw me for what I was: sharp, intelligent, with a mind for business, and offered me the position of CEO. Some people resented me there, even hated me. I heard the whispers when I walked around, but I didn't care. This company improved after I had started running things. I had five managers that I got on well with and could share ideas with, knowing that it stayed between us.

Those were the men who were joining me in the panel interview in just a few hours. The interns would be working under them, making their opinion valuable, even though I wanted to be involved in any of the final decisions. They understood that, and the process generally went smoothly, giving us a handful of new employees over the years.

I had changed a few things within the company after I had taken over, considering the internships. However, Kenneth explained the value of the program to me. It made the company look exemplary to the public, as well as offered some brilliant students who worked hard a chance for a good future, or even just experience. I'd agreed, kept it, and muddled through the interviews every time they came around. Some of the kids were still dumb as rocks, and I wondered how the fuck they did so well in school.

After I had graduated from Phillips Academy with honors, I had tooled around a little with college. I had a degree in Business as well as a minor in Accounting, because it made sense from a business perspective. I didn't have to struggle with finances or even worry about scholarships, living in one of the nicest apartment complexes in town as I made my way through the three years it took me to get my BA.

I turned the corner once I hit the main street and headed towards the gym in my building. It suited my needs without all of the bright lights and crowds that some of the others offered. I just wanted to do my routine and get upstairs to get myself ready for work.

I wasn't oblivious to the looks that I got from women in the building. I was just aware that many of them weren't what I was looking for. I was darker than most, craving control in the bedroom, and some of the younger women these days were far too feisty for my tastes. I looked for submissive women who would give in to my every need, quiet and quick to follow my orders.

I did abdomen exercises today, since it was Wednesday. I made it hurt and stayed stoic through the pain as I listened to my guilty pleasure of old eighties rap. I ran late by five minutes and cursed the elevator as I rushed into my penthouse. I showered, quickly working through my products faster than I preferred, before spiking my dark hair to perfection and ensuring that I looked like the boss that I was in my crisp Armani suit.

I met my car on the curb, a brand-new Bentley, driven by a trusted man, Mark Collins. I'd known him for years, and we had an understanding. He drove while I relaxed, caught up on work business, and enjoyed a hot cup of coffee.

It was my moment of peace in a busy day, and I cherished that drive as well as the one that took me home every time I left the building.

3

ELISA

I stood in the tiny bathroom and stared at my wavy hair with despair in my eyes. I didn't have time to straighten it and make it to Elkus Manfredi for my interview, so I reached for one of my ponytail holders and secured the strawberry blonde locks into a classic low bun, instead of leaving it down. I made sure that it was smooth on the sides before I added some black mascara to my bright green eyes and brushed a little powder over my pale skin to even it out and hopefully keep it from looking like an oil slick later in the day. I finished off with some deep plum stain on my lips, then dressed in the black pencil skirt and blazer combo with a white silk shirt underneath that my best friend Lorna had insisted that I buy when she came for a visit. It was a button up, short sleeved shirt that didn't show too much cleavage, but also didn't make me look like a nun.

I knew the truth, though. I practically was a nun. with all of the focus that I put into my schooling. I worked my ass off for the scholarship that provided me with a free ride to MIT and a little money to afford my living expenses. Mama worked two jobs just to support herself, and I'd never ask her for anything. As it was, I was working hard on my future, so that I could someday take care of her. She was fifty-five now and should be living somewhere better than one of the more run-down apartment complexes in Boston. It was my turn to pay her back for doing her best as a single mother after my father left us when I was five. Her mother helped for a time, but she was gone when I was thirteen, making Mom work long hours while she left me at home.

I was a good girl who didn't complain, working on my homework and studying endlessly. I didn't have more than a couple of close friends, but I stayed home when they went out, given our financial situation. I was thrilled when I found a tutoring job that would help to provide money to the household and worked long hours doing that after school. It was busy and chaotic, but it was my life.

It wasn't much better at this time, living with five other girls in a four-bedroom apartment. It saved money, though, so I could eat real food every now and then, and the dorms were too expensive for me. I didn't love sharing a room, but Melody was quiet, like me, and it was bearable.

I looked at the clock by my bed as I slipped my feet into my black heels and felt the nerves inside of my stomach twist painfully. I knew that I qualified for this internship and, with my teacher's assistance, I'd prove that today. I was good at school, and it felt like that was the only thing that I was good at sometimes. That would get me into this company, where I could build a future and try to get hired on. Even if I weren't studying architecture at MIT, I'd know that Elkus had a remarkable reputation in the business world. They were responsible for some of the most beautiful structures in the world and very generous to their employees. I could find myself a clean place to live, as well as one for my mother, and even see if she could be added to my benefits. I did my research once it was brought to my attention that I was one of the students recommended to Elkus, quickly realizing that it would be pathetic and stupid not to go to this interview.

I left the apartment with my thrift store purse and tossed my keys inside as I looked for the Uber car I'd asked for a few minutes ago. It was too far to walk, even if I wasn't in heels, and I'd have to cut back on something to afford rides if I got this job, at least when I wasn't in school. I could walk from there.

I saw a little yellow Focus sitting at the curb with a pretty redheaded girl looking around. "Elisa?" She asked through her passenger window, and I nodded as I slid into the back. "Where are you going?" She glanced at a screen, then gave me another look before pulling away from the curb. "Job interview?"

"It's for an internship. I'm not graduating for another year," I responded with a soft smile as she merged into traffic with a sharp twist of the wheel. I swallowed and held onto the back door as I prayed for a safe trip, knowing my dislike of cabs and other public transportation. It was a jerky ride as the girl sang along to the radio and took the turns seemingly without using brakes. My eyes remained wide and my stomach shifted uncomfortably.

"Good luck!" She told me, as she stopped in front of the massive building and grinned at me. I thanked her and got out, regretting the five-dollar tip that I'd given her on the app. That was insane. I looked up at the glass that seemed to reflect all of the light back out into the street for all to see, all the while looking flawless. I walked forward and looked into a panel near the door, making sure that I still looked presentable as I pressed my full lips together.

Entering the massive lobby, I looked for the desk to let them know that I'd arrived. The cold blonde woman, who looked almost fake, directed me to the bank of elevators and instructed me to take one to the tenth floor. From there, the receptionist would direct me where to go. I thanked her and felt her eyes looking me up and down as I walked away, aware that it wasn't in a good way. I shook it off, pressed the button, and waited with a group of similarly dressed people that split up as the three doors opened simultaneously.

I ended up with two guys and two girls who nervously discussed the interview. I remained quiet as I glanced at them and tried to decide if they were dressed better than I was and if they went to a better school. We all appeared to be the same age, and I looked away as one of the guys moved his eyes towards me. "Are you here for an interview as well?"

"The interview? Yes, I am." I smiled as I responded, and he nodded as he looked me over. It was uncomfortable, and I was relieved when the elevator stopped on the fifth floor, opening to reveal a gorgeous man who walked in and stood by me as we waited to go. The guy ogling me turned forward as I shuddered and wrapped my arms in front of my chest. I knew that I had a decent figure I should be proud of, but I didn't want others appreciating it. I glanced at the man beside me to see that he had a scowl on his face, and I wondered if he'd done something to the student looking at me.

The door opened a few floors up, and I let everyone else get off before I stepped forward. I felt shaky, and I tried to take a deep breath as the last arrival slid his hand in front of the sliding doors for me. I looked at him and murmured thanks as I looked to the left and right to see the other group going towards the middle of the floor.

It was stunning here. I wouldn't even begin to guess what the square footage was in this building, and everything inside was clean and, in some cases, sparkling. I looked outside and realized that the glass offered some sense of a tint so as not to blind you in the building. The floors were some sort of a gray marble, and I didn't see a speck of dirt on them. There were couches scattered about with tables, and not the kind just for looks. These could be used for the nap that I felt like I needed right now.

I approached the desk as the others left and glanced behind me to see the man from the elevator looking at me before he disappeared down a hallway. He was intense, though I couldn't pinpoint what it was about him. "Good morning. I'm here for an interview," I told a brunette with resting bitch face as she asked me my name in a monotone voice. "I'm Elisa Moore."

"They'll be calling you in order as the interviews move along. Have a seat anywhere in this lobby." This girl made me miss the driver's bright smile and enthusiasm.

"Thank you," I told her with my own bright smile, wanting to make a good impression every step of the way. I'd blown it with the guy on the elevator, but what were the chances of him being involved in the interview? This was a huge company and, even if I got the position, I might never see him again.

He was handsome. It was a shame that I didn't have the confidence for a man like that.

I went to sit and wait off by the window, not looking for conversation today. I checked a few apps on my phone to kill some time as I only proceeded to become more and more anxious as the minutes ticked by.

4

DAMON

I knew that I had to get back to the sixth floor for the interviews, so I pressed the elevator button and waited. As the doors slid open, I saw a group of who I recognized as potential interviewees, so I moved past them and stood beside a young woman. When I glanced over, I saw one of the men looking at the quiet girl wolfishly and shot him a dark look with my icy blue eyes. I knew what he was capable of. I didn't even look at women that way, and I was a dominant. There was something called tact that I appreciated as a man past my early twenties.

He turned and faced the doors again, and I smirked in response. I watched her out of the corner of my eye, and the woman shivered as she crossed her arms over what even I could admit was a generous chest. With a slightly closer look, I realized that she might be here for an interview. She was young and dressed in what one would term a 'power suit,' something that was common in the business world. She looked beautiful, and I turned my head as I saw her start to look at me.

Beautiful and far too pure for my kind, particularly if she was here to interview to become an intern. That was against my own rules, despite the numerous women who had attempted to seduce me here. I didn't mix business with pleasure, and I had an entirely separate place for the latter, somewhere I doubted that any of these people would be found.

We came to the floor that I suspected everyone needed, and few who were talking in their young voices and immature sense strolled out first. I sensed the other woman holding back, so I stepped to the side and gestured to keep the door open so she could exit.

Based on what I'd seen, she had more of a chance of getting any kind of position here over the others, even if she was nervous. She walked out and looked at me with bright, wide eyes that were green, held a touch of shimmer, and were highly unusual. Her pale cheeks were spotted with pink, and she blushed further as she thanked me and gave the lobby a long, lost look.

Interview. Fantastic. I could not be attracted to anyone that I worked with, and a part of me hoped that she'd blow the interview. I was drawn to this girl, something that was atypical for me at work, and it was best nipped in the bud. My imagination was already going to dangerous places with her. I wasn't known for avoiding something that I wanted if there was a strong enough need.

I joined my managers in the large conference room, and we sat in our places at one end of the table with our coffee and notebooks. I always jotted down bits and pieces of information about what made one person stand out, as did the others, so as to compare notes later. We were interviewing seventy-five students total, thirty of which were here today. I knew from experience that half would be weeded out based on the resume, most of which was provided by the school, as these kids hadn't worked yet. I dug deep into their school career, though, dating back to what they were involved in during middle school. This wasn't an intelligence contest; it was a look into who you were as a person.

Though we could all lie, couldn't we? I didn't let on to many about my extracurricular activities after hours, being the private man that I was.

We started bringing the candidates in, one by one. A lot of the applicants were young and immature, despite their recommendation and accompanying paperwork. They weren't ready for this step, and I dismissed them in my head as they each left. When the douche bag from the elevator walked in and sat down, I made a point of staring him down as his face paled. He was gone before he even had a chance.

I listened through the following three and found them to be boring. I knew that my tolerance was getting low as I glanced at my Rolex. I needed to go to lunch, or at least my office, and decompress from this nonsense.

I glanced down at my list to see that a woman named Elisa Moore was up next, and sipped my lukewarm coffee as the door opened and she stepped inside. I sat up instantly, taking in the soft pale skin and those unforgettable eyes. Elisa smiled, but I could tell that she was still scared as she sat at the table while one of us went to retrieve her resume.

I stared at her as she handed it over. Her eyes flickered over me and dread filled her face for a fleeting second. She knew who I was just as much I did her, and it turned me on to see her cheeks turn pink as I licked my lips. "Miss Moore," Brent started, as I forced my eyes to her paperwork.

Elisa was exactly what we were looking for, and I fucking hated that. She had previous job experience, and it was complimentary to boot. She'd been involved in all of the right things through middle school and high school, but still had time to earn the highest possible grades each year. She was top of her class at MIT, which was a feat in itself.

She'd be a valuable asset to this company, if only my cock weren't throbbing underneath this table. I imagined her tied to my bed and spread out for me, with her pink pussy exposed and ready.

I sensed that she wasn't entirely confident about the questions, but someone had schooled her well. She answered with the right amount of enthusiasm and what I took for a facade of confidence. That was all we needed, and I glanced around at the other guys, seeing grins on their faces. Shit. I needed to stop this before it even began. I felt a drop of sweat slide down my face as Jacob thanked her for coming, his tone warmer than it had been with the others. He assured her that she'd hear from us soon, and she thanked us, taking the time to make eye contact with each one of us, just a flash shorter with me than the others.

Elisa stood, and I watched her hips sway as she walked out of the room, feeling a strong need to push her down and bare that ass. It was tight and juicy, and I pictured her skin with marks from my hands staining it...and more. The door closed as I blinked and Ryan set his pen down. "One more like that one and we're set. Is anyone else sick of talking and hungry like I am?"

"I'll have Brynn order in sushi, and we can speak in the small room, though I think we all agree on Elisa," Brent said, as he pulled out his sleek phone and sent a text before he stretched.

No, we didn't. Maybe they didn't want her, but I did. I wanted, with every inch of my soul, to be the one to make her scream my name.

"I let Rachel know that we're breaking for lunch as well. We'll start back in a couple of hours," Ryan told us, as he stood and the others followed. I was the last to stand and leave the room, swearing that I could still smell her cherry blossom scent. Fucking hell. We went to the smaller room located in the corner of the building, where we wouldn't be disturbed. I made some coffee and sat down as I pinched the bridge of my nose to tame the headache that was forming, while the others talked about the interviews.

"Elisa is in. She's a natural for this place," Brent said, as he took a long drink from his Coke and paced the room. "Pete seemed good as well."

Douchebag. No way in hell was he working here.

"I wasn't into either of them," I said casually, as they all stared at me.

"What the fuck, Damon? She's great, and that track record is flawless. She's a hire, not just an intern." Ryan argued, as I took a sip from my cup.

"Elisa was young and Pete...seemed like an asshole," I said, as I stared at the table.

"Last I checked, they're college students and naturally younger than we are," Brent pointed out, as I tried to find someone else to bring up instead. Inside of my heart, I knew that it wasn't going to happen.

"Elisa is hot, but we know the rules here. Don't shit where you eat. She's fantastic," Ryan acknowledged, as I fought not to give him the same look that I gave Pete.

A couple of delivery guys that we knew brought in trays of food and some plates, and my managers reacted enthusiastically. I was the last to get my plate and fill it with a few pieces of sushi before I sat at the end of the table. "So, we're all on board with Elisa, right?" Ryan checked and slowly looked at me.

I had to think of the company and nodded slowly as I chewed around some salmon. Once I'd swallowed, I spoke up about Pete. "I don't want him, though. He was a dick in the elevator, and I didn't like him at all."

"Okay, he's off the list. We'll finish up today and see if we can find a second." Brent said, as he slipped another roll into his mouth. We lingered for a while in there, not wanting to be back doing more interviews. The guys were probably just tired in general. I was thinking nonstop about Elisa and what I could do to have her work here without running into her.

Interns generally worked on the fifth floor with the teams, right in the action. While the managers had offices on this floor, they spent lots of time down there, whereas I didn't necessarily have to. I could cut back how much I was down there, and it could work. Hell, I was the CEO and could send emails all day and jack off if I wanted to. There was stuff for me to do that was less involved.

The other interviews passed in a blur, and we called it quits at four o clock. They were talking about a guy named Devin who seemed great for the company and, from what I could remember, he was. I agreed just to be able to get to my office and be alone for a moment, though I wasn't certain why.

At least we didn't have to suffer through this again tomorrow. I walked in and closed my door as I trudged to the desk with my shoulders tense and aching. I needed a drink, a massage, and I needed to come and get this out of my system. I dropped into my seat and pulled out my phone, setting up a private massage in a local room that I used for such events. I headed over there to shower and pour some scotch to ease my mind. Sharon was a good masseuse and familiar with me. She wouldn't mind working naked and letting me pinch her ass before she gave me one of the best hand jobs to date. Sharon would probably do anything that I wanted her to, since I tipped so well on top of paying her fee.

I answered the door with a towel wrapped around my waist, about two glasses of scotch into the night. She gave me a curious look with her topaz eyes that were done in dark makeup. "That's quite the welcome, Damon. I can't say you're not ready, though."

I let her in and watched her move towards the bed. She lay down the thick towel that she used to protect the blankets from the oils that she used. Sharon was dressed in a tiny black skirt and boots that she removed before she placed her jacket on a chair. Her shirt was a thin tank top that hinted at her red lace bra, and I pressed my lips together.

"Take everything off," I growled, as she looked up at me with wary eyes. She looked into my face, probably to make sure I was sane and not going to turn into a serial killer on her. Her eyes drifted to my cock tenting against the towel. "I'm just incredibly horny, Sharon. I don't want to hurt you, at least any more than usual."

I could see that my words turned her on, and she removed her clothing with eager hands as she told me to get on the bed. She loved the tease of a sensual massage. I jerked the towel off and moved onto my stomach as the need to come throbbed between my legs. I smelled her oils as she slicked them over her hands, a mix of peppermint and citrus that she used to stroke my muscled back with firm hands.

Once she was beside me, working my shoulders, I reached over and palmed her ass as Sharon moaned. I gripped hard, and she fumbled against my skin before she found my neck and rubbed it firmly. I hated that I pictured Elisa standing there, and closed my eyes as I massaged Sharon before finding her clit with my hand. I wasn't normally this forward, and almost always made it about me, but fuck if I wanted to hear a woman come tonight, even if it wasn't the right one.

Sharon grabbed at me as I stroked and teased her with my thick finger, crawling on the bed to part her legs further for me as I slid a long, thick digit inside of her. She rocked against me, and I pictured Elisa with her skin flushed and her lips parted when I heard her moan my name.

She came with a wash of warmth over my fingers and pushed me over onto my back, forgetting all about the oils. "Mother fucker, what's gotten into you? Normally you're good for a hand job, after a mostly professional massage, but that? That was hot." She bowed her head over me and took my cock into her mouth as I pulled her closer by her hair.

"Eat my cock, Sharon. I want you choking on it," I murmured, as I let my imagination take over for me, replacing Elisa in every image.

5

ELISA

I heard my alarm go off too early in the morning, considering I'd been dreaming inappropriately of Damon all night. I was with him an hour tops, if you combined both times during the day, but there was something there. Every man in there was young and good-looking, but he had made an impression in the elevator even though I wasn't sure what had happened in there.

If I had a room of my own, I'd just get myself off and sleep all day, but I was me. I would go to class and do the right thing. Groaning softly, I made my way out of bed to try and sneak in a quick shower. It wasn't easy in an apartment with five girls, and I needed it after sweating all night. I rushed back into the room in a towel to pull on some jeans and a comfortable sweater, way over being modest, by now. in front of Melody. My hair was half dry, and I tugged it into a ponytail before I grabbed my backpack and headed out the door.

My phone rang somewhere in the depths of my bag as I locked the door, and I almost didn't answer it, but I remembered the interview. It was utterly presumptuous to think it was Elkus, or even Damon, calling. It hadn't been twenty-four hours, and I wasn't sure if the panel went that well, if I was honest. I had been nervous and had felt like I was babbling through the entire thing.

I didn't get calls from a lot of people, though.

I slid the bag to the ground and dug around my front pocket for the phone, not even looking at it as it rang a fourth time. "Hello," I breathed into the phone, as I struggled to get the keys into a pocket.

"Can I speak to Elisa Moore?" The voice was masculine and calm, and I tried to determine if it was Damon.

"Yes, it is," I replied, as I bent over and got everything I needed before walking to the bus stop. A car wasn't happening, even with a scholarship and a little money. My mom had a vehicle that barely got her to work at the local Walmart.

"This is Brent, from Elkus Manfredi. We met yesterday." Brent. Cute blonde guy, but not the greatest guy that I'd ever seen.

"Good morning, Brent. How are you?" I asked, as I waited anxiously.

"I'm excellent. I'm pleased to be able to offer you a position as an intern here, working with my brilliant team. You made it." He sounded happy, and I felt my mouth drop open, reminding me how chapped my lips were feeling.

"Oh sh...wow. That's wonderful," I corrected myself quickly and smiled. "Thank you so much!"

"There's the usual paperwork to be done, so if you could come in soon to sort through that, it would be great. I'd like to get you started as quickly as possible," Brent told me, as I fast forwarded through my day.

"I can drop by this afternoon. Will that work?" I asked, and I heard him tapping on something.

"Perfect. Ask for me where you checked in for the interview and we'll get you started. I'm looking forward to making you a part of my team." Brent ended the call, and I sat down on the bench at the bus stop as I stared forward for a long moment.

This was surreal. I was going to be working at Elkus Manfredi. Well, not working, but closer to that than I was before. I watched as my bus pulled up and stood up with an impulsive spin on my toes before I blushed and got on the bus with a nervous giggle. I found a seat in the middle and reached for my phone as I Googled the place that I'd be interning at soon. I clicked around their site, found staff listings, and read through the list, looking for Damon's name. I'd forgotten his last name, but he'd mumbled the first when he'd introduced himself the day of the interview.

There it was! I read down and looked at his picture for a blissful moment before my eyes widened, and I gasped. Damon was the CEO? He looked to be in his late twenties, at the oldest. I slumped back into my seat and sighed before I shook my head. A girl like me doesn't have a shot with Damon as a regular architect, much less anything else. I surrendered the fantasy that I had for a fleeting moment and kept reading about the company, as I pushed Damon to the back of my mind.

It was a good company with a great future, as I already knew. I would get wonderful benefits, were I hired, an excellent wage, and a lot of perks. I thought back to the interview and tried to recall my impressions of the panel. While they were guys in suits, they had seemed friendly and welcoming toward me, and willing to help me as needed. All of them had been talkative, apart from Damon, and I wondered if he just assisted in the decision making.

Did Damon choose me?

I watched as we approached the beautiful buildings, sat up, and took a deep breath. This internship is what mattered. My future and being able to help with my mother is what mattered. Not some school girl fantasy about Damon, who could have anyone, and probably did. Some of those girls were beautiful at the office, if a bit cold. He was probably some seductive player who could melt panties with just a breath. The idea made me laugh, and I waited until the bus stopped before I got off and followed the cluster of students onto campus.

I thought a lot about the internship and what it could mean for me during the three classes that I had that day, which wasn't the best idea. Everything moved quickly at school, and I would end up jobless if I blew school off, so that needed to stop. I forced myself back into the moment, took some better notes, and paid attention until it was time to leave for the day.

I caught the bus again to go downtown, toward the Elkus building, as I looked at my clothes doubtfully. I was just doing paperwork, and this would give me a chance to see what the dress code would be, as well clarify a few other things. It was all right to go straight from school this time.

I hoped that I didn't have to dress like I did for the interview every day, since that could get expensive.

I got off at the stop across the street from the building and walked over as I stared at it. It was exciting to think that I'd be spending my time here after all of my hard work. I glanced over to see Damon walking with a girl who had multi-colored hair in shades of blonde and brown. She looked upset, and he seemed frustrated. I watched as he swung his head around and met my gaze. I looked away and rushed into the building.

I nearly ran to the elevators, bypassing the desk this time, and slipped inside of an empty one as I watched Damon enter the building alone. The doors closed, and I jerked as it moved upward. I hoped that I'd avoid him today, at least. He was too gorgeous to even deal with.

I made my way to the desk on the sixth floor and asked for Brent as the girl at the desk once again looked me over. It was the same girl, with the same expression, making me think that it was a good thing that I wasn't here to make friends. She typed something into the computer and told me to sit down in the same chairs. I walked over and looked out of the windows, comfortable in my jeans and converse today. I felt like myself. The other day was uncomfortable, but today I was here after seeing all of the other people interviewing.

I'd made it.

Brent came out in Docker-style black pants and a blue button-up that matched his dark blue eyes. He smiled and welcomed with a handshake. He seemed casual and comfortable today as he led me to the corner of the building and into his office. It was spacious, with a fantastic view, and he watched me take it all in with wide eyes. "It's nice, isn't it? You'll have a view in the rooms that you're working in on the fifth floor as well."

"Good. I love this," I said, as I sat down in the seat across from him and smiled. "I'm sorry. This is just...overwhelming."

"You earned it. Everything about you impressed us yesterday, Elisa. You'll be a great fit here." Brent reached for a folder and smiled ruefully as he handed me a pen. There was a lot of the common information needed that I wrote in carefully, as he typed something on his computer. I noticed a section asking for tax information and asked him about it as he smiled at me. "That's for later, if you get hired. We like to have information on file."

"Okay," I replied, as I filled it out and moved on to the next paper. It seemed like forever before I was finished, but, realistically, it might have been an hour or so. Brent gave me a tour of the sixth floor and took me down to the fifth to show me where my break room was located. He also showed me where the restrooms were, introduced me to the team that I'd be working with, and gave me a badge to get in.

My schedule was based on school, so I'd be working a few afternoons and one full day on the weekend. He made sure that I was fine with that, and I loved the idea. Everyone on the team was so kind and enthusiastic, so it would be great to spend time with them, learning. There was a part of me that wanted to ask him why the receptionists were so bitchy, but I bit my tongue.

I left with a smile and hope for my future, knowing that I had a four-hour shift the following day.

6

DAMON

Sharon was a pain in the ass today. Things got out of hand the other night, and we fucked, which was something that I had started to regret. It was never my intention to go that far with her.

Apparently, she got attached in the process and suggested seeing one another on a more serious basis, which I immediately dismissed. I didn't date like that, and I had only fucked her because I was so turned on by Elisa.

Of course, the sex was good for her. I knew what I was doing, and she liked things rough, but a relationship wasn't going to between us. It had turned into a fight as I headed back to work from a late lunch, and I looked away for a moment, only to see Elisa going into the building.

Our building...one we would be sharing. She was officially an intern and, more than likely, here to fill out her paperwork. Shit. She looked younger today, and I felt my body respond. "Sharon, I have to get back to work," I said, as I looked into her angry face. "You're a massage therapist, and I seriously doubt that you've never fucked a guy before. You've had your hand on my cock since the very first time."

"You're such an asshole. I don't sleep with clients, Damon. I thought that you wanted something more with me when we did that." Sharon looked like she was going to cry and I shook my head.

"I don't do relationships at all. Not with you or anybody else," I told her, before I turned to hurry into the building. Elisa had run in after I met her gaze and I wanted to catch up with her. I threw away the idea of seeing Sharon again for a massage, but there were plenty of girls out there for that. I could replace her with another warm body. That didn't matter right now, though, because I wanted to see Elisa.

I was just walking towards the elevators and watching the door close with her inside when someone called out my name. I turned to see one of the investors approaching me with a smile, and I smiled back as I cursed him silently. We shook hands as he launched into his business, and I faked that I was intent on his every word.

We scheduled a lunch the following week to go over one of the events, and I told him to call me to remind me. I was a busy man and, in the state of mind that I was in, I could easily forget and fuck up my company.

Finally, I went upstairs and took a look around. Elisa was gone, and I resisted the urge to check Brent's office, since he'd chosen her for his team. There was a fight over it yesterday, but Brent won since he had seniority over the others. He was thrilled afterward when he followed me to my office and closed the door with a cocky smile. "She is going to rock the team, Damon."

"I agree with that. She has an impressive history." I fed him the general talk, as I walked behind my desk and looked over the city.

"I'm going to call her tomorrow and set up the paperwork," Brent told me, as I looked at him. "I want her to start."

I knew that Brent had a steady girlfriend, but I couldn't help but wonder if he was interested in Elisa. Ryan was the one who pointed out that she was hot, but Brent would have a direct link to her. I felt something inside of me that I was unfamiliar with.

Jealousy. Fuck that. I wasn't a jealous man.

We decided that Ryan would get Devin on his team, who was

right up there with Elisa, only as a Harvard student. He would be a good fit as well and seemed like he had a natural personality.

Everything was set, and I could focus on running the company, even though I wanted to focus on Elisa.

I came back to the present as I went into my office and sighed. I probably wouldn't see her too much, and this would fade away.

I tried to do some work on the computer and made a few phone calls, including taking the one regarding my upcoming lunch. Lincoln was persistent, or maybe he sensed that I was distracted. Who knows?

I stayed past six and finally gave up on trying to work. I headed out, finding the building emptier than when I had arrived. The sky was darkening as I walked out of the building and toward the car that was parked at the curb. I slipped inside and saw Mark look back at me. "Early night for you, boss man."

"I suppose it is. Take me to Bait, Mark. I need a drink." Mark looked at me, knowing that it was a club I frequented. It was a BDSM club, and, though it was no secret to Mark that I was interested in that, I hadn't asked to go there with such conviction before. I might be done with Sharon, but there was no reason that I couldn't find another girl.

"On my way," he said, as he turned forward and pulled away from the curb, I wasn't dressed for Bait, but I didn't want to go home first. I wanted to give in to the feeling that came with a woman doing anything that I asked—anything that I craved. Nothing else mattered right now.

Mark picked me up when I called him a few hours later. I wasn't drunk, but I'd say that I was tipsy. I had been in one of the more hard-core rooms tonight, and my cock ached from edging so much as I watched the depravity around me. There was a woman with her mouth around my cock while I had another bent over in just a leather thong as I whipped her with a paddle. She cried out with every hit, and I watched her come as she leaked through the edges of her skimpy underwear.

I felt out of control for a moment as I grasped the hair of the blonde on her knees before me. I started fucking her mouth in earnest as she let me slip deeper into her throat, and I pulled away to come all over her face as she looked up at me. I stepped back and went to one of the bathrooms to clean myself up as I stared blankly into the mirror. I didn't understand what I wanted here. I didn't know what I was feeling for Elisa.

The other girls weren't helping me, and I hoped that would change. I wanted to soothe myself the way that I knew worked, the way that I was familiar with.

7

ELISA

I wore my usual casual clothing to school the following day, excited about my afternoon after my last class. I hurried home to change into a casual skirt and t-shirt, since it had been approved by Brent. If we were meeting with a client for any reason, then we were to dress up a bit more, but, otherwise, it was business casual. The other members of my team wore their own styles, from gamer-nerd to alternative. There was a girl named Autumn who had rainbow hair and the best laugh that I'd ever heard in my life, and then a guy that looked like the singer from Soundgarden. It was evident to me that, as detailed and technical as architecture was, it was also another form of creativity. This company welcomed personal style, and I smiled as I walked into the work room that first day.

"Hey, girl. Good to see you," Autumn greeted me, as I smiled and looked at the group scattered around in chairs, trying to work on a design.

There was Brianne, a platinum blonde who was a new graduate from Harvard. She was twenty-three and quiet, but I thought that it might take time to get to know her. There was Vince, an unattractive guy with dark hair and big brown eyes who was obviously passionate about his work. He seemed to have an energy level that never faded, at least from what I'd seen. Landon was a surfer type who seemed subtle in his talent, but who was welcoming to me.

The last guy was Michael, and I was convinced that he was a gamer during his off hours. Though it wasn't my thing, I didn't judge people for what they did. If it made them happy and didn't hurt anybody, then they were welcome to it.

We talked as we went over the new project, which was a museum in New York City. It was going to be massive and called for a contemporary design. I already knew that their buildings cost millions, sometimes, to build with all of the detail, and these people who I now worked with did very well doing this job. Elkus was a generous company that worked hard to keep their talent, and not a person that I was watching today seemed unhappy. They seemed motivated, like I wanted to be when I was done with school and working a job.

They came down to a mutual decision, and Autumn started to draw it out as they looked over her shoulder. I sat and watched, caught up in the moment before I glanced out into the hallway and saw Brent talking with Damon, their faces close together. I stared for a moment before I blinked and looked back at the group as they pointed at something and laughed. "Come on over," Landon told me, and I smiled as I stood.

I felt like a part of them as I watched, and even suggested a few things. We had so many details about the project to work with, and it was fun to discuss, until Autumn dropped her pencil and took a deep breath. "I need a damn coffee. I was up brainstorming most of the night about this shit."

"Come on. Group break," Michael decided, as they stood and looked at me. I giggled as we went to the break room and made coffee in the Keurig one-by-one, as we talked about the city and what we did outside of work. I was the only student, of course, but they were all understanding about it.

I walked to the elevator at seven o clock, tired, but in the best way possible. I was smiling when I got in and leaned against the wall as someone slipped their hand between the closing doors. I looked as they opened again and Damon walked inside, staring at me. "How was your first day, Miss Moore?" His voice was rough, and I felt my body respond immediately as I dropped back against the wall.

"It was great. This whole place is so...enlightening," I told him, as I felt the smile taking over my face. "You can call me Elisa. I practically work for you now."

Damon looked pained as he pressed the button and we moved down towards the lobby. "Fine, Elisa. You can call me Damon as well," he choked out, as I looked at him.

"Are you okay?" I asked him, as he dropped his eyes to the floor. He was gorgeous even as pain crossed his face, and I got lost in him. I had a boyfriend in high school, and we did all of the stuff that a couple was supposed to do, so I wasn't a virgin, or completely inexperienced here. I had an idea of what was happening, but this was powerful. It was consuming, and I blinked as he lifted his eyes to mine.

"I need you to focus on your team and I need to not see you, Elisa. It's for the best." The doors opened and he was gone as I stared at his ass that was walking away from me. What just happened?

I stepped off of the elevator and shook my head. Autumn was talking to a tall guy with dirty blonde hair, and she glanced over at me. "Hey, Elisa. This is the other intern, Devin. He's from Harvard."

I stepped forward and forced a smile on my face as he reached a hand out to me. "Pleased to meet you, Elisa. I guess we're the lucky ones."

Damon's words played through my head again, and I forced myself to look into Devin's warm green eyes, darker than mine, and trustworthy. He didn't look like I was making him ill, like Damon had. "We sure are. I think this is going to work out very well."

"A few of us were going for drinks. Would you like to join us?" Autumn asked, as I thought about the low balance in my bank account.

"Maybe just one," I replied, as she grinned and led us out of the door. Devin followed us, and I felt his eyes on me as we went through the door. He was a handsome guy, and seemed kind. Maybe he wasn't a bad idea, coming from Harvard and all.

We hit up a bar around the corner, where I paid for one drink, and Devin covered the rest. I don't know if he could see the panic on my face back in the building, but I appreciated his kindness, and I sipped the cocktail as I thought about my budget. This seemed natural to them, and I wanted to be a part of the team. I just needed a few more hundred dollars in my account to keep up with them.

We left the bar some hours later, and I realized that I had spent my cash on the drink and couldn't get home. My apartment was several blocks away, and I bit my lip as I stared down the street.

A Bentley drove past me on the nearly empty street as I looked over to see Devin and Autumn slipping into separate cabs. They waved, and I smiled and waved back before I turned to start walking. I sighed and thanked my earlier self for wearing flats as I thought about the fifteen daunting blocks to the apartment. I wondered if I could just sleep at the Elkus building for the night, since it was right around the corner.

The couches there were more comfortable than my bed. It was quieter, too.

I walked and knew that the fancy car was still beside me as I stared forward. "Elisa? Are you walking?" I looked over to see a cab with Devin hanging out of it. "Want a ride?"

I looked past the cab to see the Bentley's window lower just enough for me to see Damon's simmering eyes. My mouth dropped open.

"Elisa?" I looked back at Devin and smiled weakly.

"I'd love it. I'm out of cash, but I'll pay you back tomorrow?" I offered, as Devin waved his hand and said something to the driver. At the bar, I'd learned that his family was wealthy and paying for school for him, as well as his apartment and life in general. The cab pulled over, and Devin hopped out and opened the door as I watched the window hiding Damon from the world roll back up, the car speeding off into the night.

What the hell was going on? I slipped into the cab beside Devin and closed the door as the driver asked where I lived. I told him, and he pulled away from the curb as Devin slipped an arm around my shoulder. This was a guy who was interested in me, as far as I could tell. A night at the bar wasn't deep, but he'd paid for several drinks for everyone and chatted a lot with me. I assumed that was how it worked out there, but I was too stubborn to go for it. I was focused on school and the end game, and I worried too much about my mother.

I let myself smile as we drove down the road, music playing loudly as Devin laughed at something that had happened that night. I didn't want to think about the confusion surrounding Damon, who seemed like he was in pain earlier today, yet appeared to be following me home...in a Bentley! Damon had a driver like one of those crazy rich guys who you hear about on the news, but then I remembered. He was a millionaire in the high numbers and probably close to being more. Family money and success made him a wealthy man at a young age, which was all the more reason for me to get him out of my head.

The cab stopped in front of my building, and I saw the look that Devin gave me as I looked up at him. "Can I walk you up?"

"Sure," I replied, as I slipped out of the cab and told the driver to wait for a moment.

I saw the Bentley across the street, parked with the window rolled down as Devin slipped his hand over my lower back. I felt scared inside, scared of my feelings as well as what was happening here.

8

THE INTERN INSTALLMENT BOOK 2

An Alpha Billionaire Romance

By Michelle Love

9
DAMON

I watched Elisa get into the cab with the other intern and my blood boiled as they drove away. I barked at Mark to follow them and felt his eyes on me as he started the car and pulled out onto the street. "Who is she?" His voice was low, but I knew that he was wondering why I was into Elisa, since I usually kept women separate from any other part of my life. I went to great lengths to do that most of the time, but I felt like a man obsessed as I peered through the windshield to see the lights of the car.

"An intern," I responded, feeling his gaze again. Mark was in my inner circle, and he knew my routine, so he knew that interest in an intern was something very different for me. I amazed many men when I told them I didn't fuck at work, even though we had some beautiful women there. Beauty was a requirement for me when I hired, but not for my own personal reasons. I just wanted a beautiful face greeting clients and visitors.

I can't count the number of times that the women hit on me, though. It went from casual flirtation to walking into my office to find a woman naked on my desk. People talk no matter what the company they work for, and I refuse to make any of the endless gossip a reality. I'd heard some of it. There was talk that I impregnated a woman two years ago, and paid her to disappear, as well as a rumor that I had an affair with a married receptionist and ruined her marriage.

Lies. People talked too much.

I kept my eyes on the cab as it turned and Mark kept up. I had no idea what I was going to do once this car stopped, but I had to have a glimpse into Elisa's life. I also wanted to see if the cocky intern went inside with her, a thought that made my skin crawl. I hated the idea of anyone's hands but mine on her body, and my cock hardened in my pants.

I saw the cab pull up and ordered Mark to park across the street, where I moved to the window and rolled it down to watch everything that happened. I noted that her apartment was not in a good part of town and that concerned me. I watched as Devin got out of the cab before helping Elisa out. He smiled at her as he asked something, and I leaned closer as she nodded and looked back at my car. I knew she knew that I was inside, essentially stalking her. Her eyes widened when they met mine in the dim light from the street. Elisa turned her head, and I clenched a fist as Devin placed his hand on her lower back and started up the steps with her.

Was she going to fuck him tonight? Did he expect her to?

They disappeared into the building, and I settled back into the seat. "Take me home." Mark drove away, and I closed my eyes as I tried to sort my feelings about this woman and the way that she got to me. I pushed away the image of her on her knees as the intern fucked her from behind the way I longed to do. I remained quiet as we made our way back to my house and then got out at the curb.

"I'll see you early tomorrow, sir," Mark told me as I nodded and met his gaze. Could he see that I was coming unraveled? I walked up the steps and greeted the doorman as he held it open for me, before taking the elevator to my apartment.

Looking at the clock, I realized that it was past one in the morning. I knew that I should sleep, but was feeling like a manic. I strode into my office to get the laptop that was on the desk. I brought it to my room, warming it up on the bed as I stripped my clothes off and glared at my erection. I ran a hand through my messy hair and dropped onto the mattress to log onto the computer, find my favorite porn site, and try to work this out of my system. It was a hardcore site, and I skimmed the different types of entertainment before I found the amateur category. I clicked and watched videos made by people in various settings that were rough and sometimes sloppy, finding myself stroking my cock as I watched a woman who looked like Elisa get spanked by one man while another held her still and fucked her face. Her moans around his hard cock were making me harder as I moved my hand faster and dropped my head back.

Elisa replaced the woman in the grainy video as I found myself coming closer to release. It was me inside of her mouth as she looked at me with her big eyes, swallowing the load that I shot into her throat, instead of onto my stomach. It was me who was tugging her back and driving my cock inside of her as screams filled the room.

In reality, I was alone and covered in my own sticky semen. I pushed the computer away and went to shower to put myself back together as anxiety raced through my veins. I hated this feeling, and I reluctantly walked over to the drawers at the sink and opened one slowly. There had been a time when I took pills to calm down, a time when things were too much. I pulled out the bottle and took a deep breath before washing one down with a glass of water.

I slept poorly, at best, but was awake and running early regardless of that fact. I needed to burn energy, and I ran faster, passing everyone before I went to the gym and did my kettle bells. I worked out a little harder and took another shower before choosing another suit to wear to work, making sure that my appearance was perfect. Regardless of what was going on inside of my head, nobody at my company would ever see it.

Mark was at the curb with coffee, and I sipped it as I threw myself back into my routine, desperate for normality again. It was all good until I stepped out of the car and saw the man from the night before walking inside the building, laughing with someone as he made his way to the elevator. I followed from a distance, barely saying anything to anybody as I boarded another car than the one he was on and made a mental note of his appearance. He was tall and lankier than I was, with an arrogant smile and messy darker blonde hair. I didn't see much else, but I hated the mother fucker and wanted him gone.

On the sixth floor, I got out and strode to my office. I had a list of the new interns there that I was going to check to find out his name. That was my first order of business, before I focused on any other part of my day, and I slammed the door closed as I walked to my desk.

I knew that I wasn't liked here, so the gesture didn't bother me. I preferred that they avoid me with the mood that I was in, causing me to shake another pill into my hand before I let this jealous rage take me over.

10

ELISA

Devin opened the door to the dingy lobby of my building as my heart pounded. He seemed confident in the fact that he was going to get somewhere with me, but I didn't want that, even if I hadn't lived with so many people. "Thanks for walking me in, Devin. I'd love to invite you in for a drink, but I have roommates," I told him, as he reached a hand around my waist to stop me from walking.

What was Damon doing out there? Watching us? Did he follow me home? I didn't know whether I should be terrified of him or turned on, but the latter was currently winning, and Devin was not going to benefit from it.

"How many?" He asked smoothly, as I narrowed my eyes.

"Several, since we're all in college together. Just saving some money, you know. I don't have company over," I replied, as he eyed the entrance to the lobby.

"Want to go to my place? I live alone," I knew what he was getting at, and I shook my head slowly.

"It's late, Devin." It's late, and I don't do one-night stands, much less one-night stands with people that I work with.

"Can I take you out sometime? I had a good time with you

tonight." His eyes sparkled as he shifted his attitude and I pressed my lips together. "I come on strong sometimes, and I know that. I'm just into you, but we can take this slow. How about dinner Friday night?"

I reasoned that there was nothing wrong with dinner, in theory. It was a public place, where I could get to know Devin further and see where this could go. I shouldn't trash the guy because I had some kind of weird thing for a boss that I could never have, right?

"Sure, I'd like that," I told him, as a handsome smile graced his face. I wanted it to do something for me, but sadly there was no reaction inside that didn't have to do with Damon.

"We'll talk at work tomorrow and plan something." Devin leaned down and brushed my lips with his so softly that there was barely any contact. It was a good move, but again, I felt nothing. "I'll see you to your door. " He kissed me again at the door after I unlocked it and I told him good night before I closed it and locked it.

I walked quietly through the small rooms and cleaned up in the tiny bathroom before sliding through my door and out of my work clothes. I always slept in a big t-shirt, and I glanced over to make sure that Melody was asleep. She was. I could hear the sound of the ocean waves that she preferred going to sleep to when she was alone, as well as the noise from the street below. I slipped under the thin covers and found my headphones under my pillow. I plugged them into the phone and wondered what to do with the throbbing between my legs.

I clipped one over my ear and played some classical music as I brought up the internet. My phone plan sucked anywhere other than here, where I had Wi-Fi, and I had to make the best of the situation.

I pulled my knees up and searched for erotic stories, thinking that might do the trick. I liked the books that I'd read in the past, but I wasn't about to pull one out right now. There had to be something online to read.

There! I found something that seemed to offer erotic tales, as well as a variety of something else. I chose the hottest thing I could search for and scanned the titles and descriptions, as I wondered what Damon was into. He looked like he would know just what to do with a woman, and I found a story that involved spanking before I clicked on it.

It was immediately hot, and I bit my lip as I read about the woman bent over the desk as her skirt was lifted, conveniently showing a thong. I never wore those, but it suited the story, right? I let my hand trace over my conservative cotton underwear as I devoured the words and started to stroke myself. I was careful to stay quiet and bit down hard on my lip as she was getting pummeled by his hand. I imagined the hand belonging to Damon as I was on the desk. Holy shit, what was wrong with me? I'd never even done anything close to this in bed, since my one encounter with a fellow nerd in his room during high school had been awkward and not enjoyable. It was at the point that I chose to focus on school.

God, my thighs were burning, and I slid my hand under the cloth as I moved onto the part of the story where he was taking her on the desk, all of her clothes ripped off as she clawed his back. I kept my body still, only moving my hand as my body tensed up with every press of my fingers.

Oh, God.

I came when the woman screamed his name, and was so tempted to scream out that I pressed my arm against my mouth and bit down. It hurt, but I came harder from that as I closed my eyes and remained quiet. If I lived alone, I'd do that every night. It was incredible. I glanced over at Melody, once I recovered, to see her still sleeping and wiped my hands on my shirt.

Just for fun, I read another story that made me repeat the process, slower this time and just for the release. I bookmarked the site and plugged my phone into my charger before I continued to listen to music.

I guess I fell asleep at some point, because it seemed like five minutes later that my alarm was going off. I groaned and hit snooze out of habit before I rolled over and pressed my face into the pillow.

Reality took over after the alarm went off again, and I opened my eyes to see that the room was empty. I must've slept harder than I thought not to hear Melody get up for class. I took a deep breath and stretched before standing up and grabbing my robe. I showered quickly and dressed in the usual jeans and shirt for school before I pulled my hair up into a high ponytail. I grabbed another skirt and sweater with some flats and placed them as neatly as I could into my backpack before I left for class.

I grabbed a large coffee today and blended in with the students as I played the night before through my mind again. It seemed surreal, knowing who I was. I was working at a fantastic place, with a possible future if I didn't screw up, but attracted to the boss who seemed to like to follow me around town. That was creepier than I was allowing it to be, and I tried to reason with my normally logical mind.

I needed this internship and needed it to lead to a job. That was my future, not some dream about the CEO of the company who would make all of my hard work pay off for myself and my mother. What was Damon going to do, sweep me off of my feet and make everything right in my life? No, because this wasn't Pretty Woman and people in the real world worked for what they had.

My thoughts drifted to Devin, who presented a more likely scenario. He was a great looking guy, and he was going to be successful in life. Devin was also close to my age, and it would be natural to settle into something with him as I worked toward my own career. It would be realistic, if I felt something for the guy. Would that come later, after a few dates, or perhaps a few more kisses? I wasn't stupid enough to think life was like the books or television shows, but it seemed like I should feel something.

I walked into class and sat near the front as I unloaded my notebook. I wanted to ask my mom about this, but our time was precious when we talked, and I didn't want to sound selfish. I didn't want to seem like I was ready to move on and leave her behind. She never did that to me.

I managed to focus enough to take notes, and I felt a bit more normal when I left the campus for the day. I could handle all of this and concentrate on the prize at the end of whatever twisted tunnel this might be. That was who I was and what I did. I ordered some lunch at a campus deli and changed into my other clothes in the bathroom while I waited for the food. I added some mascara and a little lipstick to my face and noticed the weird look on the guy's face as he called out my order. I blushed and took my tray to a corner table as I tried to study some notes before I went in for my shift.

Useless. I threw away my trash and shoved everything back into my backpack before I caught the bus to the office. I reasoned that, after a few weeks of doing this, it wouldn't feel so new. Going to work would just be a daily thing, where I did what I needed to do without any confusion or ridiculous attraction. Maybe I'd like Devin and have something going with him by then, something that would fit well with the rest of my life.

As I walked into the building, I saw Damon talking to someone by the elevators as he held his phone in his hand. He looked angry, and I bumped into a man because I was so focused on Damon. "Sorry," I apologized with a beet red face, as the suit looked down at me with a scowl. I looked at the floor and pressed the up button on the elevator as I longed for the floor to open up and suck me into it. As the door opened, I couldn't help but to lift my eyes to see Damon's eyes dark as he stared past me. I glanced over to see the man who I had bumped into and looked back at Damon with wide eyes.

He moved his gaze to my face and locked eyes with me before I walked into the elevator and pushed the button to close the door. I leaned against the wall and took a deep breath as I thought about the intimidating look in Damon's eyes. He looked like he had wanted to kill the guy. But why?

11

DAMON

I found out right away that the intern in question was named Devin and that he had an impeccable record, much like Elisa. They'd probably be a great couple, but I didn't want him to have her.

I wanted to have her in every way that I possibly could. I wanted to own her, but that would wreck my tidy life where work and pleasure were completely separate. I read his information again. Devin wasn't working with Elisa, or seeing her regularly, as far as I could tell. What they did outside of the office was fair game, but I didn't even want that.

Heat flooded my veins as I thought about her, and I closed my eyes.

It was possible to fire an intern, but, in this case, based on what? I'd be the laughing stock of my friends and managers if I admitted that I was jealous of a workplace relationship, something I abhorred otherwise. I always told them to never go there, and, as far as I knew, they followed my advice. He'd been here just a few days, like Elisa, and I doubted that Devin had messed up significantly—certainly not enough to be let go. I wasn't even going to go down the road of inquiring about him, since I knew how selective we were as a company when it came to bringing on interns.

I closed the screen and opened my email as I drank my coffee. I remembered that I had a meeting for lunch with a major client and was glad that I wore one of my best suits today. I knew that I needed to adjust my attitude. I had a few hours, so I spent the time in my office, not seeing a thing in my company, as I normally did. It felt antisocial and strange, and I left for lunch early just to get some air and avoid the temptation to go stalk Elisa.

I arrived early to the bistro and sat at the bar to have a drink as I waited for Stephen. He was one of the biggest clients that I had, and I couldn't blow this. We needed the income and the good word around town. The whiskey calmed me some, and I felt loose and relaxed when Stephen showed up. We headed to a corner table.

He presented the idea of several hotels all over the world, hotels that he wanted us to design. We ate steak, and I looked over the plans, well-aware that this could be the contract of the year. It would bring in millions, if not billions, and we'd be in every magazine again, earning us more clients. He was going to give me a week to talk to my managers and get together a skilled team to get things started, and we shook hands after I took care of the bill. It was an expense that I was willing to write off, given the money I was going to make. I had another drink at the bar, something I rarely did, making me fuzzy as I made my way back to the office. I ran into one of the security guards who wanted to talk about an issue with one of the security cameras. I tried to focus as I covered my mouth and attempted to make eye contact with him. I noticed Elisa out of the corner of my eye and watched as she bumped into a tall man who glared down at her as she faltered and looked up at him.

I lost the conversation that I was involved in as I glared at the man before I moved my eyes to her face. She was embarrassed, and I could see that she wanted to be anywhere else as the elevator opened and she ducked inside. I walked away from the security guard and toward the man, then felt someone grab my arm.

"Mr. James? I was talking to you." The guard looked confused as I pushed a button, slipped into the next elevator, and hit the button for the fifth floor.

I stepped out to see Elisa getting off the elevator. She began to turn left, then I called her name. "Miss Moore? A word, please."

"About what?" Her voice was quiet and tense as she looked at me and back toward her office. I stared her down until she approached me and leaned against the wall.

"Are you all right? I saw your...interaction down there," I told her, as she frowned and let out a sigh.

"Of course. I bumped into him, and he was a jerk. Nothing more than that," Elisa explained, as she looked at me with a sharp gaze. "Why did you look at him that way?"

"I hate when men treat women like that," I admitted, as she leaned closer to hear me. I remembered why I avoided drinking at lunch now and pinched the bridge of my nose as I closed my eyes for a moment.

"What's wrong?" Elisa asked me, as I heard the elevator open behind me. Glancing around, I saw that it was empty and reached out to pull her inside and close the door for some privacy. I knew that alcohol weakened me and made me lose my inhibitions, and I stared at her scared face. "What are you doing?"

"I just need a taste," I explained, before I cupped her face and kissed her soft lips. Elisa protested for a moment, then I felt her hands cover mine and she returned the kiss slowly. I reached back and pressed the button that would take me to the roof, where I found a private moment every now and then. Our lips crashed together as we rode to the top, and I heard the ding before I turned around and took a deep breath. The door opened, and I surveyed the light area to see that we were alone as I took her hand and led her outside.

I knew that I was feeling a little intoxicated and that this was a bad idea, but I needed more.

Elisa shivered and crossed her arms as she pulled her hand away. "What are we doing out here? I need to get to work, Damon. This is my job." She wouldn't look at me as she leaned against the door frame. "You're acting weird. Are you drunk? I tasted the alcohol on your tongue."

Shame filled me as I stepped back to look at her. Elisa was scared and, more than that, uncomfortable. I knew that she'd kissed me, but now she was uncertain of everything. "I had a few drinks at lunch. I saw you in the lobby, and I couldn't let you go, but I don't think that it's just alcohol. I know I need to stay away from you, Elisa. I just don't know if I can."

"I need this internship, Damon. I can't blow this chance, because I might never have it again," She stared at me, and I saw strength in those eyes. "You're not worth the risk, even if I do want you more than I've wanted any man. I have to go back to work. They'll be looking for me." I watched her turn to leave, opening the door and walking back to the elevator as I remained alone in the shade.

I felt empty and broken for the first time in my life, at least, for the first time because of a woman. They would usually do anything for me—anything for that last kiss. Elisa walked away from me, and I walked over to the edge of the rooftop and gazed over the streets at the city that I once felt like I owned.

12

ELISA

I rushed inside and pushed the button for the elevator, turning to look behind me. Did I want him to chase me and tell me that I could have him and the internship?

No, that wasn't my path. I was supposed to finish school and get the best job that I could, to take care of Mom and me. I couldn't lose sight of that because I was attracted to the boss.

I stepped into the car and pushed the button for my floor. I ran my hands over my clothes and my hair, as I tried to look around to see a reflection of myself. I couldn't look like I'd done this with Damon, whatever this was. I stepped off the elevator and lifted my head as I headed straight for the restroom to find a mirror, and whatever was left of my dignity.

When I came out, Devin was passing by to go to the men's room, and he stopped with a smile. I had fixed my makeup, and I knew that I looked back to normal, so I smiled back.

"Hey, you," he greeted me.

I compared his kiss to that of Damon's, and it was night and day. Devin's was pleasurable at best, but Damon's was like the air that I needed to breathe to survive. I know that I'd lost myself in that elevator and likely led him on, but he was intoxicating and, even now, my mouth burned for more. It felt like I would never stop tingling for him, no matter how much time passed.

"Hi, Devin. How are you?" I asked him, as he looked me over.

"I'm great. I'm really looking forward to Friday," His eyes searched mine, and I nodded.

"I am as well." I felt the sweat pooling in my hair as he looked at me and quickly licked my lips. "I need to get to my team, Devin. I'm running late today, due to traffic, and they're expecting me. Can we talk after work?"

"Sure, that would be great. Are you all right, Elisa?" He looked concerned, and I brushed a drop of sweat from my forehead and smiled.

"I'm fine, Devin. I just hate being late." There was a lot more that I could've added to the statement, but I left it alone. I didn't need to give Damon any more fuel than I already had.

"Get to your team. I'll meet you in the lobby after work, around six? That's how long you work, right?" I nodded. Normally it was, but I was willing to stay if things ran late. I already felt like I needed to make up for what I'd done with Damon. "See you soon."

I saw Autumn walking over and she watched Devin leave. "Did you guys hit it off?"

"Kind of. I'm sorry that I'm late, Autumn. There was traffic getting here," I told her, as she shrugged.

"No worries. You work hard when you're here, and this is Boston. Traffic is everywhere," She smiled and pushed the bathroom door open. "Check out the plans!! They're looking hot."

I grinned and headed to our room to greet the rest of the team. I loved it here. I loved the vibe and the creative flow that existed here. I didn't want to risk it for a fling with Damon, even if it would be the hottest thing I might ever do in my life. I needed this for my future more than I needed any man.

I looked over their progress and admired it. I longed to be a full-time employee here, doing this every day, but that would come soon. I just needed to prove myself, and I would have that.

I threw myself into the project, and we talked about ideas, jotting some down as Michael worked on the computer. Everyone had their place here, and I was going to find mine as well.

We ended up working until eight before we straggled out of there, and I knew I missed Devin. I didn't care too much, though, which was something that I didn't want to focus on. Devin was the right guy here, and the one that I should be with.

I accepted a ride home from Vince, who lived near me, and we talked shop the whole way home. I got out, went inside my apartment, and made a quick sandwich before I went into my room and read a book on my Kindle until I fell asleep. It was exhausting to have a conversation with all of the girls who lived here when we were all home, and I wondered when I'd be able to get my own place. Maybe I could get something nice with Mom, somewhere she could walk outside and feel safe.

I dreamed about Damon that night. In the dream, we didn't stop with a kiss. I let him take me in that elevator, in some alternate universe, letting him have me against the walls as I cried out his name. It was rough and intense, and I could hear the sounds of our bodies slapping together as I woke up slowly with a low moan. I pulled my hand out of my underwear and looked over, in horror, to Melody's bed, thankful when I found it empty.

I couldn't believe that I'd dreamed that and, judging from the throbbing between my thighs, had gotten myself off in my sleep. How embarrassing. I needed to figure this out and get him out of my head.

I showered and went to class dressed in a skirt and sweater for the office in order to save time. It was chilly out, but my tights and jacket took the edge off of the cold as I sipped coffee and tried to focus on class, taking lots of notes. A lot of the students used laptops, but I found that writing it down helped me to remember, something I learned early on. Most of the time I'd type them into a file for study purposes, to further the process. I had a hard time making sense of what I was writing today, and downed the last of the coffee as I frowned and looked at the board.

I grabbed a muffin before my next class and another coffee with a sigh. Everyone drank coffee all day at work too, and I suspected that I wouldn't be able to avoid the addiction for too much longer. So far, I'd just treated it as something special when I was fatigued.

When I stepped off of the bus to go to the office, I glanced around to see a coffee shop on the corner, followed by another one down the street. I laughed, and watched as the door opened to the further one and Damon stepped out with Brent, taking my breath away. He was dressed in his regular suit, something that he managed to improve with a crisp black jacket. I drank in the sight of him and realized that he always looked so perfect, not a hair out of place, or ever shabby.

Apart from yesterday. Yesterday, he'd looked a little messy after the elevator. I watched as he turned his head to look down the street, meeting meet my eyes, and everything come back to me from the day before. Even with the distance, I could see his irises darken, and his mouth soften as I licked my own lips.

I turned to walk into the building, once again pushing away my feelings.

13

DAMON

I was a wreck after I went back to my office from the roof. It took everything that I had not to go and snatch Elisa from her office and have my way with her in mine. I had the most spacious office in the building, and there were a lot of surfaces to christen, something I'd only ever wanted to do with Elisa.

Seeing her on the street made the situation far worse.

Her words played back through my mind as I tried to read through emails, applying them to my own life. I couldn't risk anything, either, since dating her would be completely against the rules. I sensed that Elisa wasn't the kind of woman to want to give it all up in order to be taken care of by me, like some of the others I'd encountered. For some reason, Elisa was adamant about getting this herself, and I knew that she had the talent. She wouldn't settle for less, something that turned me on more about her.

Elisa was different.

I left a few hours after the incident, once I realized that Brent noticed that I was on edge about something. He was one of the only people who I considered a friend, but I couldn't admit to him what was going on. I used the excuse of an appointment and ran out of the building to work out, something that seemed to keep me in control.

I worked out for an hour, noticing a redhead across the room who kept glancing my way. Her hair was a very artificial red, but she had a nice body, and I looked her over as she smiled my way. She made her way over to me once I was finishing up on the treadmill and met my eyes with her own hazel gaze. "Hi. I don't typically approach men in the gym, I swear. I just couldn't help it."

"It's not a problem. I'm Damon. What is your name?" I stepped down and still towered over her by several feet.

"Natalie. I just moved into the building a few weeks ago," she responded, as I sized her up with my eyes. She did something in business to live in this building, and I looked for a ring on her finger. I learned at an early age that a wedding ring didn't stop a lot of people from coming after me, but her hand was bare. Natalie was around my age, and I wondered about her as I looked into her eyes.

We made our way to the elevator, talking. She told me that she was the owner of a high-end cosmetic company here in town. I wasn't too familiar with that kind of thing, but I knew the name enough to understand that it was successful. She invited me inside her apartment for coffee, an invitation that I accepted as I looked around her smaller unit with sharp eyes. She was single, and everything was simple but nice inside.

We sat down at the bistro table for coffee, and I told her about my company. I saw the look that I always saw in women's eyes when I spoke about myself. She was impressed and interested, and I selfishly decided to take advantage of that as I sipped my coffee.

I let her kiss me first, but I took it from there. Her lips were nothing like Elisa's, but I pushed past that, took her to her bedroom, and tore her skimpy bra from her body after I'd destroyed her tank top. I knew going in that Natalie wasn't one of my usual kind of women, but she went along with everything that I did. She was naked before I was, sucking my cock as I forced it into her mouth from above as I slipped my shorts down. We were both sweaty from the workout, but the idea of her mouth cleaning me up excited me as I reached back to finger her clit, making her moan around me.

I remembered Elisa's mouth as I started to rock against her and closed my eyes. I slipped a finger inside of Natalie, and she bucked forward as I felt teeth on me. I pulled out and stared down at her, red-faced and breathing heavily. "Do you have a condom?" I asked her, since I didn't usually hook up with women in my own building. I didn't carry them with me, particularly to the gym.

She reached for the nightstand, yanked open the drawer, and threw something at me. Even if I didn't have my finger buried inside of her, I'd know that she wanted this from her eyes. I took the packet and ripped it open, sliding the latex over my generous cock before I told her to get on her knees. Natalie scrambled to do so, and I spread her legs and drove myself inside of her. She cried out, bucking against me as I took what I wanted and more, grabbing her hips as I moved again.

Natalie's creamy breasts were bouncing in the light of the sun as I fucked her, and I reached around to cup one, finding her nipple with my fingers before I pinched down. Natalie screamed and tightened around me as I smiled and squeezed harder. She came all around my cock as I jerked inside of her and filled the condom, my thoughts filled with images of Elisa.

I was hard even after coming, and I turned her onto her back and sucked on her small nipples as I fucked her again. She was like a doll in my arms, and I felt her release again even though she could only moan softly now. I bit down as she arched her back and shot her warmth over me, coming again in the new condom that I'd demanded.

I felt my anger towards myself slip through the cracks of my need and pulled out of the woman underneath me. A quick glance told me that her world had completely changed in a different way than mine had, as I pushed up to go to the bathroom.

I checked back through my memory to make sure that I hadn't told her where I lived in the building, or even where I worked. Natalie was busy trying to flirt while talking about herself, and I hadn't had the time, something I was happy about at the moment. I hoped she had gotten what she wanted, because it was never happening again. I could already feel my walls going up around me as I exited the bathroom and picked up my shorts. I needed a shower.

"Damon, are you leaving?" Natalie asked, as I glanced at the bed.

"I have work to do," The cold tone in my voice made its way through the room, and I noticed her pull her blankets up around her body as she shivered. I hoped that she understood that this wouldn't happen again. I had let my need for Elisa control things for a moment, and that wouldn't happen again.

"Oh." Her voice was small from the other side of the room, and I walked into the living room to gather the rest of my things before I walked out.

There had to be a way to regain control of what was happening in my life.

14

ELISA

I worked past eight and wondered if that's how this was going to happen. Was I slowly going to stay later and later and let it consume my life? Or was it just a way to keep Damon out of my mind? I took the offer of a ride home and went home to study for a test the following day before realizing that the next day was Friday and I had a date. I'd only seen Devin from a distance at work the rest of the week, but I knew that he'd find me tomorrow.

I let out a sigh and read through my written notes with a scowl, not having time to create a document this week. I sipped the energy drink that I used only when I needed it and glanced at Melody, who was hunched over her own books with some noise reducing headphones over her ears. I didn't think she ever listened to anything, sometimes, since she was so still.

I focused my attention on the words in front of me and tucked the blanket further around my body. This apartment had central heating and air, but it wasn't the greatest insulation in the world and the cold weather seeped through the walls.

I started thinking about the date and about what we were going to do. I remembered the look in Devin's eyes outside the bathroom, and I knew that he'd want more than a kiss. He was into me, more so than

I was into him. Should I just give in and let him have me? Maybe it would cure the itch deep inside of my body that all of the dreams and orgasms didn't seem to stop. It was all too easy, and I read the words on the page over again.

I fell asleep around midnight, too tired to stay awake. The light was off already, and I was using the clip-on that I'd bought at the cheap corner store. I regretted not even having my computer in the late hour, and I whispered the words to myself as questions and answered them before I gave in to sleep.

I woke up in time for a shower before I ran off to school. I hoped that Devin would give me time to come home before we went out, since I looked like every bit of the overworked college student that I was. I took my test and felt great about it as I left the classroom to attend my only other class of the day.

The other students were noticing the change of attire, since I was now dressing for the office all day. I didn't have a lot of friends, but I told them about my internship as the comments became more frequent. They were all impressed, I could tell. I wondered how many of them applied for my internship or others and didn't get them.

I headed to the office after class to get in some hours. I knew that I'd be leaving earlier tonight, so I wanted to make that up, despite the fact that I was putting in more time than required. I reminded myself that there would be a time when all of this would pay off, and I'd be at peace. Devin was walking in with coffee as I got there, and we talked on the way to the elevators, planning the night. He told me that he'd pick me up at my place at seven o'clock after I told him that I wanted to change. I agreed. I didn't think I had time to fit him into the chaos that was my life, but he was an appropriate man with whom to at least try.

I felt the afternoon fly by, and then I was leaving to catch a cab. I was starving, and relieved that the date included dinner plans, as the car weaved through the constant traffic of Boston. I rushed into a full apartment and ran to my room to put the only black dress that I had on over my other clothes before I fixed my face in the tiny bathroom mirror. I slipped on the heels that I'd worn to the interview and walked out into the living room as the other girls sat on couches and giggled. It looked like a club night to me.

"Elisa, you look so pretty! Are you going out?" One asked, as I smiled and nodded while taking water from the fridge.

"Date," I said simply, as they looked at each other with wide eyes. I was not known for dating at all, and I knew that it came as a shock to them. I glanced at the stove clock to see that it was almost time and sipped the water slowly. How I needed out of this place! There was a knock at the thin door, and someone rushed to answer it as I opened my mouth to protest. It was no use, though, so I just made my way over, pulling on my jacket at the same time.

I could see all of the girls looking at Devin as he asked for me before their gazes turned to me. I could see the questions in their eyes as I pushed forward to smile at him.

"Do you live with all of them?" Devin asked, as he led me from the building with a careful look around.

"God, no. There are a lot of friends around on Friday and Saturday nights." I felt him take my hand as he led me to a fancy car a few feet away. Devin opened the door for me, and I inhaled the scent of leather as he walked around to his side. "I prefer to get out, myself. It's too small in there, even with just the residents."

"You're not close to them, are you?" Devin asked, as he started the engine and I paused to listen. It was so quiet compared to Mom's car.

"It's just a situation to save a little money," I affirmed, as he frowned in the light from the street.

"Isn't a dorm a better option?" Devin asked, as I took a moment to answer the most common question in my life.

"This I a cheaper option, until I get a job. It's not so bad, since I'm at the office now most of the time. I just sleep and study there, and it's decent." I had practiced the response over and over, and it sounded confident and natural to my ears now.

"It could be in a better area," Devin grumbled, as I smiled at him.

"That's why I'm glad my roomies are sleeping with some of the guys from school that live there," I said, as he laughed.

"But not you?" Devin asked, as I shook my head.

"No, not me." I told him, looking forward to seeing where we were going. I was pleased when he pulled up to one of the best restaurants in the city and walked around to open my door before he handed the keys to a young man standing on the curb.

We went inside to find a crowd, and Devin led me right to the hostess stand to tell her his name. We were led to a table in the corner, where Devin checked to see if I liked wine, ordering us a bottle when I nodded.

I learned more about him over the meal, as Devin confirmed that he came from money and had a comfortable ride at school. He was the opposite of me. Once he asked me about myself, and I opened up about Mom and what our lives entailed, I saw the sympathy cross his face. I hated that, but he reached across the table and took my hand. "I'm sorry, Elisa. I can see why you've come so far."

"Have I?" I asked, as I stared at him.

"Yes, you have. You're in one of the best schools in the country, and you got the coveted internship, Elisa. You're at the top, and you won't live in that apartment forever," Devin explained, as I frowned and looked into his eyes. "You have me on your side now, as well."

"Okay," I said shyly, as I released my hand to take a bite of the salmon with a smile.

We ended the meal a couple hours after arrival. He took my hand, and we walked down the street, past some shops, as I looked in and laughed at his jokes. This was fun, even if it wasn't the heat that Damon made me feel. I could work with this.

He turned at the corner, and I found myself surrounded by apartment buildings as I looked at him. "Where are we?" I asked, as he ran his free hand through his hair and smiled at me.

"That's my building," Devin nodded towards a brownstone, and I looked ahead to see a building on the corner. He wanted me to go there, meaning he wanted to kiss me again. Devin might want to do more. I licked my lips and let him lead the way, as I tried to figure out if this was what I wanted. He was a good guy who treated me well, so far, at least. Devin was trying to understand who I was, despite our differences. He deserved a chance.

We were walking up the steps when we heard a car stop and someone clearing their throat. I looked first to see Damon watching us from his vehicle as Devin frowned. "I hope you're treating my intern with respect," Damon told him from the window, as I could see Devin try to place him.

"Your intern? Yeah, of course. I wouldn't have it any other way." Devin waited for Damon to reply, but the window rolled up, and the car drove away. "What the hell was that?" Devin asked as he looked at me.

"No idea. He must recognize us from the office," I replied casually, even though every nerve ending in my body was alert and awake. "Didn't we interview with him?"

"Yeah, he did look familiar. That's so weird," Devin said, as he looked at me. "Let's go, Elisa."

I followed him up the stairs, letting my head turn to look for Damon's car. What was he doing here?

15

DAMON

I swore off women that were too close to my personal life. I'd already seen Natalie a few times in the building and had researched gyms in the city, just to avoid her. I just didn't feel like being an asshole to her every time I saw her. She didn't do anything wrong, but I could see the look in her eyes that told me she thought that she ha. This is why I kept it to the club, to those rooms where I knew I would never see the girls outside of. I'd degrade them and fuck them sometimes, never having to make small talk or buy them a drink.

Every time that I saw Elisa in the building, I felt weak. I wanted to break all of my rules for her, even though I knew that it was wrong. I didn't speak to her when we'd pass in the lobby, but I felt her looking at me. I saw her with the other intern, and it made my jealousy rise as they'd leave together. She'd smile and laugh, but there wasn't the intensity in her eyes that I saw when she looked at me. I wanted to kill him when I saw them walking into a brownstone together one evening, his hand on her back as he helped her up the steps.

I focused on a new gym. I would not stop working out because I needed to release everything inside of me and keep myself in top form. I needed to have control, especially when I was losing it with each sighting of Elisa.

I researched her as well. She was a top student at her school, and she lived in a part of town that was not safe for her, in my opinion. I realized that they were student apartments, once I dug deeper, and assumed that she had a few roommates, but what were a group of girls going to do against someone that wanted into their lives? I wouldn't entertain the idea of a man living with her, since I considered her mine somewhere in my dark mind.

I went to the club a few times over the next week, when I had time after work. I watched as girls sucked me off, let me smack their asses with whatever device I wished, and fucked me in any position that I wanted. It felt good to walk away afterward and just go home, but it didn't get my intern off of my mind. I think it made it worse, in some ways.

I found a new gym, a very elite one that cost a mint to join. I was assured that it was a place where I'd be left alone upon inquiry, since I was only there for one thing. I didn't need women trying to pick me up and interrupting one of the most critical parts of my day. I started a new route for my jog to make sure I went there every morning, which wasn't difficult since I wasn't far. The members all seemed to be ignorant of the world, with earbuds in, listening to whatever was playing on their phones. I liked it, and I stuck to the same schedule that I did before, keeping a close eye on my form.

It was a month into the internship when I got an idea. Since it was driving me crazy not being around Elisa, why not make her my personal intern? I handled a lot of company business and could use an assistant to keep up. Brent had been telling me that for years now. She was a great addition to the team, and I had heard nothing but good things about her.

I called Brent into my office toward the middle of the week. He came in with coffee and circles under his eyes as he took a seat, and I eyed him carefully. "What's with you?" I asked, as he shrugged and set his coffee on the table.

"I was out late last night. New girl and she's younger. She has a ton of energy," Brent chuckled and looked at me across the desk. "You should really date once in a while, boss."

"I prefer to keep my life simple," I responded, as he shrugged. "So, I wanted to run something by you."

"What's that?" Brent asked, as I rehearsed my delivery in my head again.

"Things have been piling up around here for me, and I've noticed how well Miss Moore is doing with your team," I began, as his eyes darkened.

"Tell me you're not going to make her your secretary, Damon. She's at the top of her class, doing what she loves for me right now." He stared at me as I leaned back in my chair. I was prepared for this.

"I am not suggesting that at all. I merely thought that she could help me one day a week, just to clean things up. I believe that your team is the best and could spare an extra pair of hands. I've looked at the numbers." I looked at Brent as he seemed to think it over.

"Hire an assistant," Brent challenged me, as I rolled my eyes.

"I don't want someone around all of the time, Brent. Just a hand during the week with all this shit on my desk. I haven't been checking in around the building lately, because of all of this busy work." I was embellishing things a bit, since it wasn't that bad. I just wanted to be alone with Elisa and get to know her better. Perhaps I wanted to find something wrong with her, so I'd get over her. I wasn't even sure at this point. "You know that you can spare her."

"I suppose, but you've never been all that interested in the interns before this. What gives?" Brent looked at me with a frown on his face.

I mentioned the new client and some of the upcoming meetings that I had and his eyes widened. "I need someone on this, just to keep up with appointments, research and things like that. We're growing, buddy. There's going to be money in it for everyone before you know it."

Brent left excited and promised to send Elisa in to discuss the idea with me later in the day. I grinned as he closed the door, letting my mind fill with ideas about her, none of which had to do with work. I'd play the game while I tried to get inside of her head and see what she was made of. I wanted to know her desires and try to see if I could make them come true, and I stroked my cock under my desk.

I checked my upcoming appointments and worked my schedule around them, jotting down reservations that needed to be made and notes for meetings with my managers. Admittedly, I did need an assistant, but not just anybody would do. I needed her, at my desk, so I could see her and smell her. I longed to taste her again, and I stood after a while, walking over to the window after an hour of sitting.

I went for coffee after that, needing to loosen my muscles and perk up. My floor was quiet, with business being conducted with clients behind closed doors, as opposed to teams working out in the open. I thought back to the days when I was down there, just watching and learning, when this was Kenneth's job. It was exciting and hands on, but I was excellent at what I did for the company. I was in the right place and earning a lot of money.

I made coffee in the machine and stirred in just a bit of cream and sugar. I wasn't much into coffee, at least not when I wasn't thinking too hard about something. My rigorous schedule of early mornings and exercise made me sleep well once I was in bed, though, lately, I'd been thinking about Elisa.

I walked back to my office and stepped inside, loosening my tie after I set the cup down on the desk. There was a tap at the door, and I called out for the person to come in, having left it cracked.

Elisa stepped inside, dressed in a flowered pencil skirt that clung to her curves and a button up gray blouse that grabbed one of the colors. She looked beautiful as she tossed her hair back and bit her lip, making me hard all over again. "You wanted to see me, sir?"

That word sent all of the blood rushing to my groin, as I sank down into my chair to hide what she was doing to me.

16

THE INTERN INSTALLMENT BOOK 3

An Alpha Billionaire Romance

By Michelle Love

17

ELISA

I was so nervous as I walked towards Damon's door. My hands were shaking, and I could feel the sweat pooling in my hair as I mentally tried to pull myself together. I didn't know what he needed—just that Brent asked me to stop by his office on a break.

What could it be? Was I going to be let go? I couldn't be. As hard as it was to be close to him, I needed this job for a secure future for my family. I hadn't done anything too wrong, apart from trying to distance myself, like he seemed to want me to do...like it seemed was best. What was I doing here?

I noticed that the door was cracked when I approached it, and I took a long, deep breath before knocking. Here goes nothing. He told me to enter, and I pushed the door gently and stepped inside.

This room was huge and featured a large cherry wood desk and a wall of windows. The view looked to be incredible, but I was distracted by the man walking across the hardwood floor to the desk. Damon was dressed in his daily black slacks, but missing the suit jacket. He tie hung around his neck, and I couldn't help but stare at him.. I watched as his eyes widened before he dropped into his seat and took a deep breath.

I nervously shuffled for a moment and cleared my throat. "You wanted to see me, sir?" The order of things was confusing to me, as my head swam and I tried to focus.

"Yes, I did. Please, have a seat,"

Damn.

The desk was neat, apart from a few papers spread out and I suspected that he liked order in his life. The whole office was that way, and I took a slow look around as I sat down and licked my lips. I noticed that he was quiet and looked back at him to see what he was doing.

Damon was staring at me, and I tossed my hair nervously as his eyes narrowed. If he was going to let me go, he needed to just do it. He needed to get it over with and let me leave as I cried, not knowing that to do. I knew that was dramatic, but it felt real to me in that moment. "Sir, if you could just..." I let my voice drift off as he blinked at me and I blushed. "I'm sorry. Take your time."

"Damon. It's Damon. Don't call me sir," he muttered, as he tensed behind the desk. "I called you up here after a conversation I had with your manager, Brent. I spoke to all of the managers, as I regularly do, to check progress." I felt my heart drop. Brent didn't appreciate my hard work, and I was going to be let go. I tried to figure out what I had done as I stared at the wall past Damon. "I like to see how the interns are coming along, and Brent had nothing to say but affirmatory things about you, Miss Moore."

I was shocked at his sentence but focused on the use of my name. "It's Elisa," I reminded him, as he stared at me. "That's good to hear. Thank you." I waited, more curious than before.

"I am a stubborn man and don't ask for help enough. If I do, the person has to be the best, and it's come to a place in this company where I need a little assistance. I am meeting with more clients than ever, famous and high-paying clients who need my full attention, as Elkus Manfredi continues to grow. It is because of this that I asked about the interns who were most recently hired, Elisa." He made my name sound painful to say as he spoke. "I did not have in mind a full-time assistant, but just someone on a semi-daily basis to help out with appointments, phone calls, and emails. I need help with the tasks that take up the time that I could be using to promote the company. That is where you come in."

I looked at him, not understanding what he was getting at.

"I would like you to assist me, Elisa. I like what I've seen, and I trust Brent implicitly in his review of your work."

"What about the team?" I asked worriedly, as he took a breath and leaned back with a tired smile.

"You'll be working primarily with them. I'll need you for a little time during the week, but I understand what your internship entails. I know that you want to be part of a team later in your career, and I'd never interpose with that. I just need a little help, and I think you're right for the role."

"I'm flattered," I said, though shocked was more the word I would use. This had never been a thought in my mind, and I blinked as I watched him trace his tie with his hand, lost in the movement.

"There are perks to the job. I am going to be logging the hours that you work for me and pay you the going rate for an assistant, since it is a separate entity from the internship. You'll also be receiving an iPad that you can take home with you at night, a new cellular phone so that I can contact you, and access to this office and the programs that you'll be using both on your iPad as well as my computer. I trust that you can keep company business to yourself, seeing as you'll be getting a much deeper look at things, though I'll have something for you to sign, if you accept my offer."

A paid job? I knew that it wasn't full-time, but it was something to put away, to help my mom. It was too much to think about, and I opened my mouth before closing it again. I wondered how I could work with him, given that my underwear was already dampening, just from sitting here. I needed to move past what happened with us, and this might not be a great idea, particularly since he had said that he wanted distance from me at some point. This was a great opportunity, as well as a chance to stay on with the company. "Wow, that's a lot to think about. I...I think I'd like to do that. I'll take you up on your offer."

He seemed to be surprised, but soon nodded and reached for the papers on his desk. "These are for you to fill out. I had my lawyer look them over, and they'll cover all of the bases."

I scooted forward and took the pen that he offered as I moistened my lips and started with the first document. It was standard, apart from the document that he'd spoken about. I was asked to stick to a strict confidentiality rule and tell nobody what I saw and learned in here. "That includes the other interns whom you might consort with outside of the office." His words were cold, and I looked up to see him staring at me with a burning gaze as I blushed.

"Of course," I murmured as I remembered seeing him on the street that night. Not only was I his intern now, but I was also his assistant. "I'd never consider telling anyone anything." The papers clearly stated that any example sharing information could be followed up with legal action, if the consequences were severe enough, and I couldn't have understood the message any clearer.

I went back to the usual paperwork, surprised to see that he'd be paying me twenty-five dollars an hour as a part-time employee. That would add up, even if the hours were on the lower end of being part-time. I signed the last page, and he asked me to come around the desk, so he could show me a bit of what I would be doing.

We went over the programs, and I jotted down the passwords in a private note app on the phone that was charged and ready for me. I would see his emails and appointments and have control over them, something which scared me. I assumed that anything that was not company information would be located elsewhere, since Damon was clearly an intelligent man.

He was close to me as he pointed out things I would need to know, and I smelled the spicy scent of his cologne as I fought the shivers that were threatening to take me over with every word and brush of his skin. Damon was all man and complete sin wrapped in one. I jotted everything down and read back through it, trying to avoid looking like a fool on my first day. He seemed to have faith in me, so I could have confidence in myself as well.

Damon explained the devices that I'd be using for him, shocking me when he said that I could use them for personal use, as long as it wasn't illegal or a threat to myself or the company. He insinuated that he could look into that at any point, but I wasn't sure just what he meant. I wasn't smart enough to be some type of hacker, and I didn't look up much on the internet either.

I remembered the stories I'd read that one night, earlier this month, as well as a few others I'd read when I'd had some alone time. I had my phone for that, but was that what he meant? People openly read Fifty Shades of Grey, so was something online and unedited considered wrong? I decided that it didn't matter, since I had my own phone and the fancy new one was for work purposes.

Damon directed me to a document that indicated what meetings needed to be set up, as well as appointments. "Why don't we start with these? If they give you a hassle, remind them what company you're representing. If that doesn't work, use my name. They should be very compliant after that."

"Yes, sir...Damon. I will." I looked at him. "Want me to do that in here, while you're working, or will it bother you?"

"Feel free to stay in here. There's a small table over there if you'd like to use it." Hell, yes I would. It was about ten feet away from Damon, and, after all of our closeness, the distance would be appreciated. I felt my attraction to him in every part of my body, and I asked him if he'd like coffee. I was dragging and already exhausted. "I'll go with you. Those cups can be hot," he said, as he stood and put his body on full display just to torture me.

We walked to the break room quietly, and I felt the stares of the few employees who saw us. What kind of rumors would there be about me now? I wanted a job based on my effort, not how I worked with the boss. I didn't want to be the company slut, and the thought plagued me as I fixed my cup and added the proper sugar and cream to it. "What's troubling you?" Damon asked, as he closed his door with a distinct click.

"I don't want to be talked about. I don't want anyone to think that I'm getting special treatment from you," I voiced my concerns, as he looked at me and nodded slowly.

"I try and repress that kind of activity around the building, Elisa. I will remind of and enforce that rule with all of my managers, as well as the rest of my staff, but there is always a little chatter in a company this size. Try not to let it get to you, since you know yourself better than anybody else," Damon suggested, as I stared at him. I was always the wallflower and didn't attract attention, apart from school, so this was new to me. "I've heard it all, and I'm sure some of the rumors have spread your way, but I assure you that they aren't true."

I left that evening uncertain of anything but willing to try and work with the new arrangement. Devin sent me a text asking me to have coffee, but I begged off with the excuse of studying late that night.

18

DAMON

I knew that Elisa could handle the position, though she seemed nervous at points during the day. She was a skittish girl and seemed concerned with what people thought of her, something that was confirmed after we went for coffee. It angered me that a woman as smart as Elisa would let that bother her, and I had meant what I had said about handling the situation. I wanted her comfortable and, oddly enough, happy. That didn't generally concern me.

I wondered about that as I played back the day through my mind. She was scared and beautiful, with her full eyes and occasional inability to speak. I wondered how innocent Elisa truly was, as Mark stopped by a deli for my dinner. I was in the mood to be alone and dismissed my chef for the night, too wrapped up in my own thoughts for a big meal.

I entered my apartment and sat at my table to eat as I remembered the scent that Elisa wore today. She preferred sweeter scents of floral and fruit that made me want to nibble at her skin before I reached her thighs and tasted her thick honey. I was used to women who wore the expensive perfumes that turned my stomach, but seemed to impress others, though I was confused as to whom. They were always too heavy, and Elisa smelled more natural to me.

Her hair smelled like coconut and vanilla, and I longed to touch her soft curls. I wanted to pull them hard as I played with her and made her come hard, seeing a new side of her. What would she look like? The idea tormented me as I showered and rested in my room before looking over the reservations I'd given her to make today. Elisa had done well and deserved a reward, even though I had already started logging her time with me.

I chose her number from my sleek phone and paused for a moment as I checked the time.

Damon: I'd like you to keep Friday night at six free, Elisa. Let's celebrate your new job.

I sent that to her business phone, knowing that it wasn't my style at all. I had a reservation for one of the best seafood places in town and had made it with the idea of taking her out. This seemed like it was moving fast on some level, though it was moving slower, physically, than I was accustomed to. It was altogether different.

Elisa: Damon?

Damon: Yes, it is Damon. Will you join me for dinner?

Elisa: I have plans, and was under the impression that you wanted to quell any chance of rumors.

I wondered if they were with that maddening intern, and I thought over my answer before I sent back some shitty comment to her. I had to be careful now, given the choice I'd made to hire her.

Damon: Cancel them, if at all possible. I don't have a lot of free time, and this is supposed to be one of the best seafood places in the city, if you like that kind of food. It recently opened. Don't worry about any rumors. The building empties early on Friday.

Elisa: I'll see what I can do. Thank you for the invitation.

I set my phone down and considered her answer as I watched the moon shining against my wall. I knew that she felt something for me. I also sensed that there was a deep sense of responsibility in her that would drive her to do the right thing, for whatever reason. I needed to see her out of the office, over a glass of wine. I needed to figure Elisa out, if only to find a reason to stop this obsession from growing.

I was up early to run through the chilly streets, liking the temperature drops as I moved steadily through the lessening crowds. The only thing that stopped me were blizzard conditions, and I reminded myself to further consider a gym and make a choice with that.

I did my usual route, taking the long way home, where I did a few exercises to replace my usual gym time before I showered. I felt inclined to jerk off in there, with all of the thoughts of Elisa in my head, and I came to the image of her on her knees before me, baring her ass, speckled from my hand. It wasn't enough, and I told myself to get through the day and see what else I needed later.

I dressed in a black suit and a light blue shirt, with a darker blue tie. I slipped my shoes on and met Mark at the corner, sipping my coffee and checking my texts before my emails. Nothing from Elisa so far, but it was a bit later in the evening when I asked her to dinner. We had an understanding where I'd contact her if I needed anything early in the day, keeping in mind her other obligations and sticking to her schedule of afternoons on Monday, Wednesday and Friday, at this time. I wasn't going to fuck up my company or her internship, even though I knew that I'd happily have her in my sights all day long. I had to be sensible about this.

I arrived and went to my floor, giving a cold look to anyone who I felt looked at me with anything but fearful respect. I did greet them, but it was with a warning in my voice, before I disappeared behind my office door. I prepared for some upcoming meetings, getting together facts and figures to impress my possible clients and bring in more money. I knew that I didn't need it personally, but it was good for the company, something that I took pride in.

I had my phone on for notifications, as always, and sitting on my desk while I typed and saved documents. I couldn't help but wonder what Elisa was thinking about Friday, and, since this was Tuesday, there was a chance that I wouldn't see her. I got up to make some coffee, cursing my growing need for the drink that I'd disliked for so long. It was a break and a chance to walk around to loosen my muscles, as well as one to see what was happening on my floor.

It seemed calm today, and barely anyone made eye contact with me, not even the newer receptionist who had been blatantly flirting with me before this. She was an attractive woman, but lacked anything else that I wanted or needed, and I was glad that my actions this morning cooled her off.

I went back to the office and checked the company accounts, pleased with where we were. There were the usual positive write-ups in the business papers and websites, and the earnings were impressive. Kenneth would be proud of me, and I smiled at the idea.

He was a good father figure to me, after losing my own dad too young. I wasn't the spoiled brat that never wanted my mom to date or marry again, holding onto the memories of my family. I cherished them, but I wanted her happy, since she was just in her early thirties at the time of his death and still quite beautiful. She deserved a second chance at love and life, and I never stood in her way.

Now, she was traveling to some of the finest places in the world while I had control of one of the best companies in the world, one that was growing by the moment. I was guaranteed to be rich enough to live my entire life well, doing whatever I wanted.

That thought was killed by the sound of a text coming from my phone, jerking me back into reality. I snatched it from the top of my desk and unlocked the screen with my fingerprint to read the script.

Elisa: It turns out that my plans fell through on Friday. Does your invitation still stand?

Damon: It certainly does, Elisa.

Elisa: What should I wear?

Damon: I've found everything that you've worn here to be appropriate for the evening, thus far. Use your best judgment.

I sat back, pleased with myself as I thought ahead to the night. I was accustomed to wining and dining women, the ones who were worth the effort. It wasn't often that I did this, but I had both the cash and connections to make it happen Friday night.

I wasn't sure what I was doing, but I wanted more on this woman. I made some calls and left for lunch, pleased with my efforts. I noticed the intern, Devin, leaving with a group as he laughed confidently, unaware that I was tearing down whatever it was he wanted with Elisa. He would never be able to do what I could for her, Harvard brat or otherwise.

I wondered if he had seduced her the other night, touching the body that I wanted to claim as mine. I glared at him and stopped walking, until he turned to look in my direction and I turned to leave the building. I hated him, and I needed him to let me go about my business.

I didn't need to trouble myself thinking of him with her, since Elisa was going to be very much mine, starting now.

I ate at a classy Italian place as I thought about Elisa and Friday night. I knew that pursuing an intern, or worse, an employee, was against every rule that was set up in the company. It was wrong, but she was worth the temptation, and it was my business to run. I could do whatever I wanted.

Elisa was arriving when I returned to work, dressed in a lovely dark green wrap dress that brought out her eyes, with the same pair of heels that she always seemed to wear. They were sexy, but worn, and I grinned as I slowed down and watched her board the elevator. I took out my phone and sent her a text, waiting for a reply before I got on my own car.

Elisa: You need my shoe size? Why?

Damon: Just tell me.

Elisa: Size 9, but I don't know what you have in mind, Damon.

I grinned and stepped into the elevator, along with a few more upper-level employees. I greeted them with a smile and they glanced at each other for a moment. They must have thought I was bipolar sometimes, but I wasn't, and it didn't matter to me what they thought. I was used to shoe shopping for my mother, since she loved them, and I took great pleasure in sending her gifts.

I went to the website of her favorite store and did a little searching, finding several pairs of heels that I liked, but settling on two. I knew where she lived and found it to be a terrible area for her to live, much less one to send the finest of items to. I wondered about some of the properties that Kenneth owned as investments for a moment, knowing that he could afford less rent on some of the smaller properties. Hell, he could afford for Elisa to live for free in one of the apartments. They were fully furnished, and I could tell her that it was an employee perk, something that was true for relocating employees. There was normally on a time limit, but I knew that she'd be safer there, closer to work.

Closer to me.

I considered it as I gave the store her phone number in an email, so they could request her presence at the store. It would be a special moment that I wished I could see.

This was going to be so enjoyable. I scooted forward to start looking at apartments.

19

ELISA

I was leaving class the following day, dressed for my job in a plum colored pencil skirt and black blouse with a beautiful lace collar. As the weeks had passed, I had found things at some of the local thrift shops to wear and, so far, was very pleased. They were well-priced and looked good, and I wondered if Damon liked them. Shit. Damon was my boss now, and, even with all of his intensity, I knew that I shouldn't play this game. Going out with him on Friday was idiotic on my part.

My phone rang, and I pulled it out, realizing it was my work phone. I wasn't even due there for an hour. I answered it, not recognizing the number as I paused on the walkway and moved to the side. A woman with a friendly voice told me that she had something for me at one of the most impressive stores in the Boston area, and I frowned for a moment. "I don't shop there. It must be a mistake," I assured her, as I wondered what the hell was going on. Nobody had this number—nobody but Damon.

"I assure you that this is yours, Miss Moore. If I were you, I'd hurry down here because these are beautiful. Have a great day, and ask for Andrea at the shoe counter."

I looked at the phone and shook my head. Shoes! He had asked for my shoe size, and I narrowed my eyes. What was he trying to do to me? I knew that he had money and could probably get any woman that he wanted. I stalked forward to the bus as I let anger rush through me.

This was my life. This was my future. I could handle it by myself, without his help and whatever game that he was playing.

My anger was still high as I stood in front of the building, and I took the elevator to the sixth floor. I wasn't due in Damon's office for a few hours, and I knew that the team needed me, but Damon needed to be put in his place. I walked toward his office, noticing the look on the receptionist's face as I ignored her.

I had noticed that my current shoes were wearing down, but still. There were discount shoe shops, and I could get my own.

I was just approaching his door when it opened, and he stepped out, causing me to crash into him hard as I squealed. "Elisa, are you all right?" Damon asked, as he held me in his hands and stared into my flashing eyes.

"Why is Macy's calling me to tell me to go to the damn shoe section?" I demanded, as he looked around warily before pulling me into his office. "What did you do? What are you trying to do? You're my boss now, very literally and I—" my words were cut off with his kiss, as he pressed me against the locked door and tilted his head to take advantage of my shock.

I found my arms sliding around his neck as I pulled him closer and returned the passion in this embrace. My anger melted, and I turned into a needy woman as I felt him press harder against me. I lost all sense of reason as we kissed hungrily and only came back to reality when he lifted me and started to carry me across the room.

"Damon, we can't do this," I told him, as I pulled away and struggled to breathe. He was just lifting me off of the floor enough to carry me, and I felt my body being lowered to the couch. "You're my boss... I'm your employee...I'm your intern. We can't do this."

"I don't give a fuck what you are, Elisa. I haven't wanted a woman the way that I want you in my entire life," Damon said, as he pressed his body against mine. "I want to buy you shoes when yours are worn.

I want to take you to dinner and learn who you are. I want to touch you more than anything right now." He looked over my body at my carefully chosen outfit and leaned in for another kiss. I couldn't push him away, and he molded his body over mine as he ran his hands over my body and up my sides to rest just under my bra. Our lips met hungrily as he kissed me and I kissed him right back, our tongues dancing together as he slipped his thumbs over my sensitive nipples.

I jerked when he slid the shirt from the skirt and then moved his hands up my bare skin. "I'm supposed to be with the team," I whispered, as he gave me a small break in order to find the front clasp of my bra and unhook it. "Damon, this is so fast."

His eyes went hard when he stared at me and he cupped my bare breasts as I let out a small moan. "Is it? Did you fuck the other intern the other night when I saw you going into his house?"

"Oh, God...Damon. No," I pushed his hands away and tried to think as he leaned down to kiss my neck. "I didn't. He kissed me and tried to get me to sleep with him, but I wasn't ready. He's not you." He pulled away and looked at me as I took a deep breath. "I agreed to see him again because it seemed like the right thing to do in everyone else's eyes. He's a great guy on paper, but I haven't been able to think about anyone except you since the first time that I saw you."

"Elisa," Damon said, as he kissed my neck again and moved down my chest. His mouth was hot and eager as he found my nipples and sucked slowly. I moaned and slipped my hands into his hair as I closed my eyes and gave in to the feeling.

We parted before things went too far, realizing that I needed to be elsewhere in the building. An obscene amount of time had passed, and I dressed quickly and dashed into his bathroom to check my appearance. I fixed my clothes and pulled my hair into a low bun before replacing my gloss. Damon asked me to come back after three, and I agreed as he kissed my cheek with a hungry look in his eyes.

I floated into the team office and greeted them with a smile as I wondered if I was insane. I didn't stop Damon; I encouraged him. I knew that stopping us today wouldn't last, because he set my body on fire. I knew that I was risking everything by being with him.

I just wanted him, though, and nothing else mattered.

Brent popped in and told everyone that I was assisting Damon with a few top clients in the afternoon, but it wouldn't affect my work with them. I nodded and forced myself back to reality as they all gave me curious glances. Once Brent was gone, Autumn cleared her throat and looked at me again. "I'd watch that. He's...something."

"It's just an extension of my internship. Don't worry about me. I'm seeing a guy at school anyway." I made up the lie to reassure them and smiled. Inside, I suspected that she was referring to the rumors and felt angry inside that Autumn believed that. She seemed so down to Earth and invested in her job.

"It's not a bad opportunity," Vince chimed in, as I gave him an appreciative glance. "Maybe he's not as bad as we all hear he is."

There was a long silence before everyone gathered around the table again. Once we were back on subject, it was easy to fall back into a rhythm, and I sighed in relief as I felt the passion for design fill the room.

We worked until lunch, and I watched as most of the team headed out to the streets to get something to eat. Vince lingered behind, as usual, and gave me a smile. "Don't worry about them. The boss has a reputation around here, but it is an excellent opportunity for you. I mean that."

"Thank you. I didn't think it was a bad thing to learn about the business side of things," I admitted, as I stood and looked around. "Want to grab a sandwich with me?"

We walked to the corner deli and ordered before taking a seat to eat. "So, you're seeing someone?" Vince asked, as I looked at him and nodded. I had to stick with the lie now. "Is it serious?"

"It's new and casual. I'm in school and essentially working here, so I don't have a lot of time for a relationship." I saw something cross his face and realized that Vince was interested in me. I didn't notice before, but he was staring me in the face, and I thought back to the rides home and just the general conversations.

"Weren't you seeing someone here?" Vince pressed, and I licked my lips.

"That was brief, but yes. I ended up with this new guy during that time, and, to be honest, I find dating at work a bad idea in most cases." I tried to let him down easily, since Vince was such a nice guy. Nobody had a chance, since I'd seen Damon, something I willingly admitted to myself now that we'd started. I knew that it was risky and that I might pay hell for this, but I knew that I wanted him.

"You're right. I know that, but I liked you when we met. I thought, maybe ...?" Vince smiled, and I saw that he wasn't devastated. We finished lunch and walked back, feeling lighter and laughing before we made our way back to the team. They seemed better, too, and we joked and worked through the day, until it was break time.

I went to make a cup of coffee and glanced at the clock. I was due in Damon's office, and I felt my heart leap into my throat as I nibbled on my lip. This was cleared by Brent, and it was all right. "I'll see you guys later. I'm going to go help out." I smiled, and they nodded as they said goodbye and walked back to the office. I grabbed my stuff and went to the elevator to go to the sixth floor.

I stepped out and walked to his office, without the anger from before, tapping on the closed door before he invited me inside. I opened the door and found a woman leaning over his desk as she pointed at something on his computer. She was a few years older than me and beautiful, and I leaned against the door and took in the scene. "Thank you for your opinion, Caroline," Damon said, as she giggled and stood, revealing her short skirt and slightly unbuttoned shirt.

"Sure thing. Anytime," she responded, as she looked at him, and then at me, before she left the office. I felt the surge of jealousy as I wondered what the fuck I was doing with him. The door shut behind me.

"Come in further, Elisa," his voice broke into my scattered thoughts as I stared at him and took a breath. Every look that my team had given me today played back through my mind, and I could hear Autumn's words all over again. "Elisa," Damon's voice was sharp as I blinked and watched him stand and walk over to me. Damon was gorgeous, powerful, and beyond my wildest dreams. He cupped my face in his hands. "What is it?"

"Have you had sex with her?" I asked in a whisper before he covered my lips with his and reached down to click his office door, locking me in. Damon claimed me in this kiss, hard and slow as he pressed me against the wall behind me and pulled me against him. My thoughts scrambled together, and I reached around his neck to hold him close as he kissed me senselessly.

Within moments, I was back on the couch, and he was sliding my skirt up with his hands as I shuddered underneath him. I wasn't even sure how much time had passed, or what was happening, until I felt him cover my needy clit with his mouth as his tongue circled me slowly and torturously.

I came with a sharp jerk of my hips as I cried out his name, reaching down to grab his hair, unconsciously, as he drank me into his mouth. "Oh, Elisa, you're as sweet and as hot as I knew you would be. I can't wait to have you wrapped around my cock as I fuck the ever loving hell out of you." There was a darkness to his voice as he spread my legs and traced me firmly with his finger. I jerked again and bit my lip as new sensations flooded my body, the beginnings of a second powerful orgasm.

We rested on the couch afterward for a while, and I looked at him. "Was that to distract me from the question?" Damon rolled his eyes and looked me over slowly.

"You're going to push things with this, aren't you?" I watched as he pushed himself off of the couch and walked into another room, looking surprisingly together, considering what we'd just done. He returned with two bottles of water and handed me one before walking over to his desk. "Do you want a rundown of my sexual history, Elisa? Are you ready for that?"

"Probably not," I responded, before I adjusted my clothing and sat up. I took a deep breath. "I know it's quite different from mine." His eyes were sharp as they looked at me, and I opened the water, sipping it gratefully.

"You're not a virgin, are you?" His voice was low, and I shook my head slowly.

"No, but I'm not experienced either. I've slept with two men, both in college," I admitted, as he raised an eyebrow and considered this.

"So different than what I'm accustomed to, Elisa. Why do I want you so much?" Damon seemed to be asking himself that question more than me, and I remained silent as I watched him look at the seat that I was standing beside meaningfully. I sat as he stared at me in wonder. "Maybe not."

"What do you need?" I asked him, as I tried to recover from what just happened. "I mean, today?"

"Have you ever come like that before? It looked to be intense," Damon observed, as I smiled and looked at the floor.

"No. I didn't know that could feel so good. I think I believed that it was...gross, before now," I admitted, as he nodded. "I suppose you'll want me to do the same to you." His eyes darkened as he nodded and I licked my lips. "Don't you want more from me now? I mean, you didn't get anything from that."

Damon chuckled and looked out of the window for a long moment. "There's so much more to this than that. Forget those college boys who were looking to get off, Elisa. This is going to be different than that was. This is going to be so different."

20

DAMON

I instructed her on the emails that I received daily as well as attempted to return in the same twenty-four-hour period. I made a list of the most important clients and gave her free reign in setting up appointments for me, using my calendar application on my computer. It was a tedious process, but it should be easier once she adjusted to it. I made Elisa understand that she didn't need to answer any questions regarding the company, or what we were looking for right now. Those issues could be forwarded to my personal email, which I made sure she had saved into her contacts on her phone. She looked at the account that I'd set up for her assistant purposes and smiled.

Sweetelisa22@gmail.net.

"You chose this?" She asked, after I'd given her the password information, which hinted at the things that I wanted to do to her.

"I did. It's true, based on my new knowledge of you," I told her as I watched her blush beautifully. I had wanted to take it so much further earlier, making her hold her release as I teased her hot cunt and taught her control. I wanted to be able to make her come with a whisper, but I had to have her come in my mouth this first time. From there, I would make myself take stricter control with my own discipline, making her who I needed her to be. My mind wandered as I thought about this being exclusive with the two of us. Could I give up the spontaneity of the club, where I could have whatever I wanted with the snap of my fingers? I glanced at Elisa as she looked at my calendar and smiled at me, asking if it was okay to set up a lunch meeting.

I could sure as hell try for this shy, beautiful girl. I could mold her into what I needed, making her a regular part of my life. I could teach her to please me.

"Go ahead," I told her, as she filled in the day of the meeting and time, as well as where we would be meeting, before emailing the possible new client back with the same information in a friendly and professional manner. She already knew how easy it was to get a reservation in my name and dialed the number of the restaurant from the information on Google, making the reservation with a polite thank you as she looked at the computer.

"How do you get in so easily? From what I've heard, these are nice places. Everyone says it's hard to get in." Elisa looked at me as she spoke, and I felt myself harden as I stared back at her.

"I run the biggest architecture firm in the country, Elisa. It came with an excellent reputation before I stepped into the position, and people want to impress me because of that. They're willing to do anything to please me," I explained, as she frowned for a moment. "Is there anywhere that you want to go?"

"I'm not a part of this world. I eat take out on the corner for excitement," Elisa told me, as she paled and looked at my desk. "I don't want to spend my money on one meal like that. I need to spread it out."

I sensed that she struggled with money by the scared look in her eyes, and it made me want to give her a raise, as well as speed along the process of a new apartment. I had dated casually before, and treated the women well, if they were a regular part of my life, but never with the need that I was feeling now. "You're not spending your money. I am, and I have plenty of it, Elisa."

"You do?" She asked, and I nodded, leaning in to brush her lips with mine. She melted against me, and I stroked her full lower lip with my tongue as she moaned softly against my mouth. She was so pure and sweet. I slipped my tongue against hers and started a make-out session that reminded me of being a teenager with a curfew, not that had ever kept said curfew. It had driven my mother insane, but once she was remarried, she had seemed to settle down.

I pulled away to let Elisa take a breath, noting the bright pink spots on her cheeks. Elisa seemed flustered as I looked her over and jumped as my phone rang. "Should I?" Her voice was hesitant, and I shook my head, leaning over to grab the cordless.

I handled the question smoothly and ended the call with the receptionist before I set the phone on the desk. "I don't expect you to answer my phone, unless I'm not in the room, Elisa. I need help with the client meetings and scheduling mostly."

"Have you ever been involved with an intern before?"

I shook my head. "Never. I haven't dated at work for some years now. That's a program that my stepfather began, and I kept it, since it helped both the company, as well as the students who were hired. We're selective, and you know that we only pick the best of the best." She smiled and blushed again, and I took a slow breath to control the need flowing through my veins. I must be crazy, taking her in this way when she drove me mad inside. "It leads to great opportunities for some of them."

"That's why I was so excited about it. I need this on my resume," Elisa spoke with a reverence that made me curious to know what was going on in her life.

"I want you to tell me all about yourself over dinner on Friday. I want to know what makes you tick," I told her, as she stared at me with wide eyes. "For now, I just want to taste your lips." I kissed her again as she moved closer, eager to give in to me. I dragged it out, keeping the kiss deep and slow as I felt her come apart in front of me. I knew what she wanted as she whimpered against me and my fingers itched to rip off her clothes and take her right there on my desk.

I jumped as I felt her hand slide between my legs and touch my erection gently. Elisa had no idea what she was starting as she stroked me with her fingertips and met my tongue with hers. I tensed my thighs as my need grew inside of me and placed my hand over hers, forcing her against me. "Do you feel what you do to me?" I asked her softly, as she nodded. "I want your mouth wrapped around me, Elisa. I want you on your knees as I fuck your mouth."

"Oh, God," she said, as her eyes darkened and she licked her lips. I watched as she moved to the floor and stared up at me with an eager gaze. This was moving faster than planned, but she was so willing with me, and, fuck, if I didn't want to come right now. I stood and leaned against my desk as I loosened my pants and dropped them around my ankles. She looked me over, seemingly intimidated by my size, before she leaned forward and kissed the tip of my cock gently. I sucked in my breath as my body hardened toward her naturally and she circled me with her tongue. My hands slid into her hair with a gentleness that I didn't feel as she opened her mouth and took me inside. Fuck, she was so hot, and her mouth tightened around me as I closed my eyes.

"That's it, Elisa." I slowly rocked my hips as she adjusted to me and felt myself in the back of her throat. "Relax and take it all, baby. That's it." I imagined her tied up in my bed, as she moved her mouth. I gripped her head tighter as she gasped. "Harder, Elisa. I want to feel you."

Elisa moved harder, and I rocked against her as I held her still, telling myself to not come yet, as much as I wanted to. I was feeling the pressure deep inside my balls as I cried out her name with each thrust. "Coming—I'm coming," I told her, as everything went black and I shot inside of her mouth. Elisa gripped my thighs as she struggled to take it all, with my hands holding her tightly as I released. Nothing had felt like this before now, and I stumbled back as I stared down at her.

What was happening to me?

"Was I not good?" She asked, as she wiped at her mouth where traces of me ran down her cheeks. I could tell that she was shell-shocked, but still upset that I didn't like it. I dropped to my knees as I reached for a tissue from the box. I wiped at the corners of her ruined mouth, noting the tears in her eyes before I leaned closer to kiss her nose.

"You were...perfect," I assured her, as she smiled and relaxed against me. I sensed that she needed that, that she felt bad about herself, even with all of her accomplishments. I wanted to know who had made her doubt herself, if it was even a man, to begin with. Was it a parent issue, or worse? I stroked her hair, messy from the encounter, as I tried to put it back into place and heal her.

I was getting in too fucking deep, but I knew that I couldn't walk away from her now.

We left the office separately in a couple of hours, cleaned up and looking as though nothing had happened between us. Regardless of my intent with the rumor mill, I knew that the immature ones would still talk, whether or not they were warned not to. I watched from the elevators as Elisa left and met up with her team, smiling and laughing naturally, as if we hadn't done the things that we did together. She walked with Vince, and I wondered if there was anything between them as something very unfamiliar reared its ugly head again.

Jealousy.

21

ELISA

I kept a neutral look on my face as I walked out, carrying the bag from Macy's in one hand. Damon had surprised me in the office, after I was seated and recovering from him, by presenting me with the shoes that he'd purchased for me. They were heels, sexy and expensive. One pair was black, with the famous red bottoms that screamed Louboutin and money, as well as a pair of gray Jessica Simpson shoes. They were both beautiful, and he promised me more with a soft kiss at his door before he shooed me away with a reluctant gaze.

We didn't have sex, but we'd done more than I was used to. I had given clumsy blowjobs before now, that didn't end with completion. They were just a quick step, leading to equally awkward sex that apparently paled compared to what my body had experienced in that office today. I still felt his tongue between my legs as I got off of the elevator and walked over to the remaining members of my group. "How did it go?" Vince asked, as he smiled at me and glanced down at my bag. "Shopping?"

"There was a sale, and I had a break," I smiled as I thought back to the bathroom in Damon's office. Every hair was in place, and my makeup was perfect. I looked like I hadn't done so much as kiss him, much less anything else. I was covered, if I didn't blow it on my own. "Today was good. I think I'm going to learn a lot about the company this way. Who knows? Maybe I'll run one someday myself." I forced myself to laugh, and he joined in before asking me if I wanted a ride.

I accepted and told myself that I had to find a way to thank him. I knew that Vince lived near me, but it still took up his time to drop me off every day. When we were walking out of the door, I glanced back to see Damon staring at me. I fought a smile.

We chatted as we drove, mostly about the project. Vince told me that we were all up for bonuses for this project, including me. The company found ways to reward the interns for their hard work, and I bit my lip as I thought about the pay that I was getting for helping Damon. That was enough, wasn't it? I felt my face heat up, and I thanked the sky for darkening early these days.

I got out at the curb and thanked him again before walking into my apartment. A couple of the girls were arguing about a class in the living room, and I crept by quietly on the way to my room. I longed for my pay to be enough to get a place of my own, but the idea almost made me laugh. It would be in the ghetto, probably, where my mother lived and that was hard enough to stomach. At least living here, I could help her out some while going to school. I glanced at the other bed to see Melody sleeping, surrounded by books. I smiled gently at her.. I felt the same way after letting Damon have his way with me, as well as working so hard to please me.

I dressed in some leggings and a long-sleeved shirt, to fight the chill in the room, before crawling underneath the covers. I couldn't stop thinking about him and parted my legs underneath the covers as I stroked myself over my clothes. I was still sensitive from hours earlier, and I smiled as I slipped my hand down my pants to touch myself. I didn't need any words to get off tonight. I had Damon's tongue against me in my memory, and his teeth dragging against me as I came so hard in his mouth that I blacked out for a moment. It was intense and wonderful, and I imagined him inside of me, sliding that thick cock inside of my tight body, as I stroked harder. I could imagine how he would feel as he took me on my back, or maybe my knees. What did he like?

I remembered the way the woman looked at me as she left his office. He had never answered me when I inquired about her, but something deep inside told me that even if he had, it wouldn't matter. I saw something in his eyes and face that made me think that this meant something to him.

It might be better if it didn't, but, as I bit my lip and came, I knew that I was falling for him in some way.

I woke the next morning to the alarm, rolling over with a yawn as I glanced at the window. I had only the one class today and then it was off to the office, a thought that made me smile. In just a few days, it would be Friday, and we'd be at dinner. Was that a date, or just an honest celebration? He could afford to eat out every night, so money wasn't the issue, but from what I'd seen online, the restaurant was fantastic. It was where everybody wanted to be, and he got in with just his name.

Who was Damon, apart from what I saw every day? Did he have siblings? Was he close to his family? What was he doing with me, someone younger than him and clearly just starting life? What did I even have to offer?

I slowly got up and showered before staring into my closet. I found a pair of clingy purple slacks and a deep gray turtleneck sweater that would match the shoes perfectly, dressing in the ensemble before I left for class. I wore a new-to-me pea coat, in a dark metallic gray, to keep warm and walked down the street slowly, feeling like a new woman.

I grabbed a coffee on campus and made my way to my seat, thankful for just the one class today. I could spend quality time with my team and learn some more today, since I didn't have time scheduled with Damon. Did I wish that I did?

I made my way to the bus after class and rode it into the city as I watched out of the window. My iPad and phone were tucked in my worn messenger bag that I carried now, just in case I needed them. I didn't use them at home too much, since I didn't feel like they were really mine, and I had my personal cell phone for whatever I needed. Our wi-fi connection was spotty in the house, at best, which made getting homework difficult. I rolled my head back to massage my sore neck as I watched the bus approach the stop at which I was getting off.

I walked up to the building as I noticed Devin walking inside and stopped, allowing him time to get to the elevator. I hadn't talked to him, but he also hadn't contacted me. I assumed that Autumn told him that I was seeing someone at school, and he was likely confused about that.

I remembered back to the night we went to his place. Seeing Damon in his car had thrown me off, but I wasn't in the mood for Devin to begin with. I couldn't find anything too wrong with him when I thought about it. He was handsome, intelligent, and he had a great future. Devin was also funny and kind, and I might kick myself later for letting him go.

His kisses were nothing more than pleasant, though. They didn't fill me with the desire that Damon's did, or the urgency to feel more. They actually repulsed me a bit, since they came off just like the guys that I'd slept with. He seemed like he'd leave the moment I gave in, and that worried me, considering that we worked together. I didn't want that hanging over my head, so what was I doing with Damon?

Us not working out could affect everything, and I knew that seeing the boss was foolish, particularly for an intern like myself. I would always have my degree, but being let go from a company like Elkus Manfredi, especially with a reputation, would be stupid. I could blacklist myself, and then what? Mom would never have a better life, and I would've wasted the years in school and all of the hard work. I thought of her and sadness filled me as I realized that I could completely disappoint her.

I blinked and made sure that the coast was clear before I walked slowly across the lobby to the elevators, pushing the button as I looked around at my surroundings. They still took my breath away, regal and beautiful as they were. I couldn't believe that I worked here, even now.

I'd gone over some of the previous designs with Damon as he told me about the company, and they were impressive. It was something that I'd love to do for a living. I could see why he was so successful and famous around the country. I just didn't know where I fit in, if at all.

I was relieved when the team seemed busy and distracted as I walked in. Setting my stuff down, I joined in with them to discuss the plans. I was already having doubts, and I didn't need judgment with it to make my veins any colder.

22

THE INTERN INSTALLMENT BOOK 4

An Alpha Billionaire Romance

By Michelle Love

23

DAMON

I knew that it wasn't my day to work with Elisa, and it was killing me. I chose her to work with me three days out of the five, because I didn't want to get addicted to her, but fuck if I hadn't failed at that already. I picked up my phone and pulled her number up, staring for a moment before I set it down. I asked myself, yet again, why I was pursuing her, and my cock answered me as I bit my lip.

Elisa would be my finest reward, once I'd fucked her. I was going to turn her world inside out and hopefully move on with my life after that.

Still, though, there was something about her that more than just the way she enticed me sexually. She seemed genuine and kind at heart, which was a trait that I was not used to in a woman. Most of the notches on my belt were after something much more than a night, knowing that was I was wealthy beyond their imagination, and could get them far in this city. Elisa didn't ask for anything, and was even annoyed by the gift of her shoes. I'd never argued with a woman over a purchase before Elisa, and wondered where her intense pride came from.

I heard my phone vibrate on the desk and reached over to see that it was Sharon. I hadn't heard from her in a while, and I thought back to the last time that I'd seen her. I hoped that she wasn't looking for a relationship, still, but I could use a massage to ease my tense muscles. I sent her back a text, making my needs clear, even as something nagged at me in the back of my mind.

She was agreeable to a massage, and I agreed to meet her in a few hours at the hotel. That was it; just a massage. I was horny as hell, but it wasn't just for anybody. I made an excuse with my managers about a doctor's appointment that they probably saw through, since I rarely went, but I didn't have to worry about it, since it was over email. I was the boss and could do what I wanted, though I didn't feel that way right now.

I felt weak, and resented the new emotion.

I locked my office and made my exit at three o'clock, stepping out of the elevator as I started across the lobby and froze. Elisa was walking with Vince, holding a coffee as she laughed at something that he said. She looked sensational in deep purple pants and a clingy sweater, and I smiled as I looked down at the gray shoes that she was wearing. I knew she liked my gift.

Her face turned, and she looked at me with expressive eyes. I felt like shit, going where I was, but I didn't owe her anything. Still, her eyes beckoned to me before she looked forward and walked toward the elevators again. We had to play it off. I walked across the lobby, feeling eyes on me as I left the building, and walked over to the car where Mark was waiting. "Early day?" He asked, as I climbed into the back.

"I have a meeting. Drop me at the hotel," I told Mark as I caught his eyes in the mirror. I almost always had the window down that separated us, unless I had a woman in here with me. Mark could probably listen if he wanted to, though I was confident that he had his own life to worry about. Mark was a good-looking man and kept himself in shape, seeing that he was something of a bodyguard if the need arose. It was a requirement for this job, even though I could take care of myself just fine. It was just reassuring to have back up, since I was well-known in this city. Mark was a friend to me.

He pulled away from the curb and drove the few blocks to the hotel, pulling into the circular driveway to drop me off.. I told him I'd call if I needed a ride later, and he nodded as he gave me a look. "Are you okay, Damon?"

"I'm all right, Mark," I assured him, as I smiled stiffly and walked into the lobby. Inside, I felt torn up as I made my way to the elevator bank and pushed the button, staring at the ground. Something was different today. I unlocked the door and showered, slipping on some lounge pants as I poured a drink at the bar. I paced the suite restlessly before going over to my phone and picking it up, staring at the screen. I was just sending Elisa a text when there was a knock at the door, and I watched as it sent before I put the phone down with a sigh.

I opened the door and let Sharon in, looking at her in the tight leggings and white shirt. She appeared more like a professional massage therapist today. "I didn't know you owned clothes like that for work," I told her, as her eyes darkened and she walked by, her head held high. Perhaps she had dressed like that in the beginning, but I couldn't remember now. I sensed that she was going to have an attitude, and I almost sent her away, but remained silent as she covered the bed with her towel. "Why did you call?"

"I missed seeing you, Damon. You've been a client for a long time," she replied, as I realized that she was right. I'd been getting massages from Sharon for a couple of years now. She was a good girl, and, as long as she knew her place, I'd keep her around. "I apologize for the last time we spoke. I lost myself for a moment, but I know what this is now."

"What's that, Sharon?" I asked, as I strode forward and stood behind her.

"It doesn't go past that door, and I'll have no expectations," she explained, as she stared forward.

"Good girl," I responded, as I dropped onto the mattress and kicked my pants off. As far as a massage, it felt good. Sharon's hands pressed into my muscles as I tensed a few times, and my cock was even at half-mast, though I didn't want to ravage her like before.

"You're tense. Is everything okay?" Sharon asked, as she stroked my neck firmly.

"Work stuff," I mumbled, as she continued to rub my skin. The oils were slick on my skin, and I closed my eyes, imagining Elisa doing the rubbing as I felt myself harden against the towel. Her hands on my body would be so hot, and I smiled as I felt Sharon move to my back, kneading as I relaxed into the bed. I was so into my fantasy that I believed it was Elisa that slid her hands over my ass and between my legs. "Fuck," I groaned, as fingers teased my balls and stroked slowly, slick with oil.

"I knew you wanted it," the voice was garbled as I lifted my hips and allowed access. The hand tightened around me as I moaned and rocked as someone encouraged me to roll over.

"Elisa, yes," I moaned as I moved onto my back, ready for her.

"Who is that?" I opened my eyes to see Sharon staring at me with hurt eyes. "Are you seeing someone?"

"Get your mouth on me, Sharon." My voice was firm, and she licked her lips before crawling over me and bobbing her head over my cock. She moaned with the movement, and I pulled the bun out of her hair to hold her still as I rocked against her. I heard her protest as I started to fuck her in earnest, needing the release. "Take it. Swallow my come," I ordered, as I watched her move over me.

I shot deep in her throat as she gagged slightly, pulling away to stare at me.

"Is that all?"

"Finish the massage," I told her, turning over on my stomach and closing my eyes. A part of me felt badly, deep down inside, a place that I'd never had feelings before. There would always be a part of me that was dominant and got off on women doing what I told them, but perhaps I was getting more selective now.

I'd come hard.

Sharon finished the full body massage before she left, accepting the bills I slipped into her hand as she prepared to leave. She took her towel and stuffed it into the bag, closing the door behind her as I took a deep breath. I knew that she was still feeling the pain from before, since I could see it in her eyes. I couldn't find it in myself to care. I just wondered why I got so involved in the fantasy with Elisa.

I remembered the text that I sent her earlier and strolled over to wash my hands, grabbing the phone to take it to the bed. I knew that the oil was still on my skin, but I paid a lot for this room, and they could wash the sheets. I opened my messages and saw that she'd responded about fifteen minutes after my original message. Elisa was shy, even with her words, and I smiled as I glanced down to see my cock hardening again. I skipped the message feature and dialed the number, smiling as I heard her voice on the other end.

"Damon? Are you okay?" Her voice was filled with concern, and it filled me with something stronger than lust.

"Just thinking about you," I responded, enjoying her giggle. "Are you still at work?"

"We quit early tonight. Vince had a meeting," she replied, as I narrowed my eyes.

"Is he interested in you?" I asked her, as she gasped on the other end.

"What?"

"You heard me," I growled, suddenly angry as I sat up. "Has he shown interest in you?"

"I turned him down, Damon. Everyone thinks that I have a boyfriend at school," Elisa told me, as I ran a hand through my hair.

"Do you know how beautiful you are?" My voice softened, as I dropped back against the pillows. "Do you see it?"

"I don't see what you see," she told me softly, as I longed to show her in every possible way. "I don't know why you're even pursuing me."

"I want you, Elisa." I didn't call women on the phone. I didn't have conversations with them once I had slept with them, and rarely before. Elisa was different. "Where are you?"

"Home. I have to study," she replied, as I slid my hand down my stomach.

"Are you alone?" I could hear the rise in my voice as she went silent on the other end.

"For once, yes," she replied, as I closed my eyes. "I don't know how long."

"Are you in bed?" I asked, as I heard her shuffling around.

"Yeah," she said, as I gripped myself.

"Touch yourself, Elisa. Tell me how wet I make you," I said, as I stroked myself slow and hard.

"I...Damon. I've never done this over the phone," Elisa sounded nervous as I listened carefully. There was some shuffling and then a breathy moan. "Oh, God."

"There you go," I murmured, not wanting to scare her. Elisa was new to a lot of things, and I needed to take this slow. "I'm so hard right now. I wish I could slide my cock up and down your wet pussy." I heard her cry out and smiled, knowing that I was getting to her. "It is wet?"

"Yes, oh, yes," she whispered as I heard her moan again. I kept the talk going as I stroked myself, timing it to the orgasm that I knew she was close to having. "Oh, Damon. I'm...oh!" I clenched my hand tighter around myself and shot into the air as she moaned uncontrollably on the other end. This was so easy, and I jerked as my heat dropped on me.

They'd have to wash the comforter now.

24

ELISA

I felt heat wash over my skin as I pulled my slick hand away from my body, listening to Damon come on the other end of the line. It was incredible, and I closed my eyes in the room as I wondered what the hell was happening to me. I wanted to come again, and my fingers moved over my sensitive nub as I dropped my head back. I was lost in Damon, and I stroked myself as I let out another soft cry, timed with his moan. "I can't stop touching myself. I can't get enough, Damon."

"I want to taste you, baby. I want that sweet clit in my mouth," Damon told me, as I moaned again. "I want your legs spread wide before me."

"Uh...oh," I stammered as I felt another wave wash over me before I jerked back and bit my arm to keep quiet. "Ouch!" I whispered as I stared at my pale skin.

"Are you okay?" Damon asked, as I laughed.

"I bit myself. I was so into that...oh my God," I marveled, as his low chuckle filled the phone.

"I'll kiss that all better tomorrow in my office, unless you want to join me tonight," He teased, as my eyes widened. "I can have Mark come and get you, and then me. I just finished a meeting."

"What kind of meeting can you do...that at?" I asked as I blushed.

"One that is over. Should I send him?"

"I have class," I told him, as my mind raced.

"Bring some stuff. He'll take you to school," Damon suggested, as I agreed and told him the address.

"I know where you live," he said as I blushed again. "I'll see you soon."

I rushed around the tiny room, cleaning up in the bathroom before I hurried back into the room to pull on some jeans and a pink burnout t-shirt with a hoodie over it. I threw a pair of leggings and a tunic into my school backpack, as well as a few things that I'd need after a shower.

What was I doing? I couldn't spend the night with my boss when we'd be working together the following day. This was too risky, and I dropped on my bed as I took a slow breath. Everyone would find out, and I'd be talked about all over the building, which was the least of my worries. I might lose the internship.

I heard his voice inside of my head and stood again. "I just need to get him out of my system, and I'll be okay. This will end." I pulled my backpack over my shoulder and left the apartment, locking the door behind me before I approached the curb. I saw the Bentley parked and running as I approached, and a man stepped out of the driver's seat and held the back door open for me. "Hi," I said nervously as he looked me over.

"Miss Moore. We'll be picking up Damon, and then be on our way," he said to me in a professional voice, even as I saw the concern on his handsome face.

"Thanks," I replied, as I slipped inside and let him close the door. The seats were soft and buttery, and I sank back with a sigh. There was a bar in the car, as well as a music system that was better than anything I'd ever seen in a house, let alone a car. It was an absolute luxury, and I buckled the seat belt as we pulled into traffic.

The windows were dark, as I already knew from previous sightings, and it was exhilarating to know that nobody could see me in here. I'd stare at this car and wonder who was inside of it, if I were driving beside me, and I looked around to see if anyone was doing that to me. It was too dark to see. I wondered what else I could do in this car, noticing the blackened window that separated me from Mark. My imagination ran wild, and I leaned against the glass to see as we pulled into a driveway and parked in front of what I knew to be one of the best hotels in the area. I wondered again about his meeting, and how Damon would be able to do what he did over the phone here.

God, I hated my insecurity.

I heard voices and then the door opened before Damon slid inside. His eyes were hot on me as he moved over and kissed me hard, taking my breath away. I wrapped my arms around his neck as he nestled closer to me, kissing me into a state where there was no rhyme or reason—just want. A part of me knew that the car was moving as I wrapped my legs around Damon and moved over him, our tongues dancing together wildly. He pulled away and stared at me with crazy eyes before he withdrew my arms from around his body. "Which arm?"

I held up my right arm, and he slipped the sleeve up, staring intently at my pale skin with the clear mark of my teeth. He leaned in and kissed it, as promised, and I stared at him as my heart tumbled loosely in my chest. I fell a little harder for him in that moment.

"You did this for me." His words were soft as he stared at me before kissing the skin again. "Does it hurt?"

"No," I replied with wonder, as he slipped a hand into my hair and kissed me again. We made out the entire way to his place, and I jumped as the car stopped, embarrassed by what I'd been doing. My lips were tingling, and I laughed as he smiled and kissed me again.

Damon opened the door once I was put back together, and I glanced around at the apartment complex that we were at. "Is this yours?"

"I live in another place, but I wanted to show you something," he said, as he took my hand and led me into the pretty courtyard that featured a waterfall and small pond with a lot of plants. He turned right and pulled a set of keys out of his pocket. He opened a door and pulled me inside as he turned on a light. It was a spacious apartment with a sunken living room and modern kitchen. The furnishings were modern and clean. "Do you like it?"

"It's beautiful," I replied, confused. There was no possible way that I could afford something like this, unless I worked several years at the firm.

"I want you to live here," he told me, as I stared at him in shock. "It can be included in your wage, and it's already furnished."

"Damon, you must be insane. This is too nice for me," I protested, as he pulled me closer for a slow kiss.

"You live in a shit hole right now, Elisa. It isn't safe, whereas this apartment is. You could live on your own and have privacy, and it's close to work," he told me in between soft brushes of his lips.

"I can't afford this. I only work part time for you and intern the rest of the time," I protested, as Damon lifted me and carried me down the hallway. He kissed me the entire time until my ass hit a mattress. I looked around. The bedroom was gorgeous, with a big picture window and a big bed centered against the wall.

"This is one of two bedrooms. The other is upstairs, with a balcony, and is slightly bigger." I felt his lips crash against mine as I pulled him closer, lost in his mouth. I knew that I was in trouble as he removed my sweatshirt before kissing my neck thoroughly.

"Why are you doing all of this?" I asked, as he pushed my shirt up and found my nipple under the lace of the bra with his mouth. "Oh, Damon."

"I don't know," he admitted, as he unhooked the front and pulled it to the side, sucking me hard into his mouth. I dropped my arms, and he pinned them as he worshiped my body, edging me closer to a release with long draws of my skin between his teeth in between kisses. When he finally let my hands go, I ripped my jeans down myself and spread my legs open as I stared at him. "Do you want this?" Damon asked me in a husky voice as he moved to stand, staring at me.

"I want this more than I've wanted anything," I promised him, as I felt a tear slide down my cheek. I knew that he couldn't see it since there was only a little light coming from the living room and some moonlight shining through the bedroom windows high on the wall. All sense of logic left me as I struggled to breathe, all concern over my job and future gone. I just wanted him, buried inside of me, as deep as he could go as I came around him. He lifted his shirt off, and I stared at his muscled abdomen in awe before lowering my eyes to see him slip his pants down slowly. God, he was so hard and thick, making me remember the moment that I was on my knees before him.

"Touch yourself," Damon told me, as he dropped before me on the mattress, holding himself in his hand. I was scared, but reached down to finger my needy clit as I watched him stroke himself slowly. "Are you on any birth control?" I nodded as I got lost in the sensations coursing through my body. "I want you bare. I'm clean and get checked regularly to make sure of that. I never have sex without a condom, but I need to with you. I want to feel all of you."

I knew that I was insane, but I needed him and I'd agree to anything. He watched me masturbate for a few moments longer before he dropped down and drew my legs up to his shoulders. Damon positioned himself in front of me, sliding in slow and deep as I cried out his name. He filled me as I reached for his waist to pull him deeper. Every thrust stretched me, making me wetter as he drove himself in and pushed my legs back, making me moan his name.

I wanted to think about the risk involved in this as I was pressed back against the pillows hard with every movement. I wanted to reflect on his past and my future, but all that was in my mind and body was a need for Damon. Hot and wet, I needed him. I pressed my feet against his chest as I grew closer to the release I'd been craving since seeing Damon for the first time.

It was as good as expected, and possibly better, as I arched my back and screamed his name. Every nerve ending reacted as my mind went blank and I exploded around him, tightening as he drove himself in deeper and cried out my name. Everything sounded disjointed to me as my body seemed to temporarily leave me, and I came to moments later, with him beside me, breathing heavily with wide eyes. "What just happened?" I asked weakly, as I ran my hands over my skin to make sure that I wasn't dreaming this.

"Magic," he responded, as he dropped down and faced me. "Fucking magic."

I thought back to the rest of the night; the phone call and rushing out to find his car. I thought about what we did in the car together as I looked around this room in shock. This place didn't belong to either of us, and we'd just had sex in this room. I blushed, feeling guilty as he moved his hand to turn my face. "What is it?" Damon asked me firmly, as I licked my swollen lips nervously.

"It's just that...this isn't your place or mine," I started to say, as he soothingly stroked my damp cheek.

"I want it to be yours," he said, as I shook my head. "Let me explain, Elisa. My stepfather, Ken, was the first CEO of Elkus Manfredi. He's a wealthy man and invests in complexes such as this, as many do, for financial reasons. This particular one is used for new employees who may be moving from another area and need some time to find a permanent place, which I see you doing in some ways."

"I am just an intern who gets paid for part-time work, work that is done with the man I just slept with. Oh, God," I cried, as I covered my face. "This isn't who I am."

"I never thought that you slept with every man who employed you, Elisa. You've worked your ass off to get where you are, and this fucking pride that you cling to so tightly is beyond me. Don't you think that you have a better chance of keeping a job at the firm?" I looked back over at him as a tear slid down my cheek. "Hard work pays off."

"Will anyone there see that? Will they think that I worked for anything, or that I seduced the boss to get higher in the company, or, worse yet, to get taken care of?" I asked brokenly, feeling all the pleasure from the night begin to fade. I closed my eyes as he covered my body with his, fighting the pull as he held my face and stared at me.

"You never asked me for anything, Elisa. Do you know how many women have tried to seduce me for my wealth or what I could do for them? I've never offered any of this to anyone before." He told me, his eyes hard as he held my arms against the mattress.

"Why me?" I asked, as searched my face with a stunned gaze.

25

DAMON

I looked into her scared, innocent face as I tried to find an answer to her question. I was still reeling from the way it felt to be inside of Elisa, and I felt my cock harden again just looking at her body. "I..." My voice faded off, as I kissed her, partially to stall for time, and partially from desire. She kissed back, fighting to release her arms as I held them so I could claim her mouth without interruption. Her tongue was eager against mine as I moved her legs apart and placed myself in between them.

Elisa moaned as she lifted her hips, making me stare down at them as I pulled away. "Please," she asked, as I slid forward and inside of her. I knew that she was slick with both of us as I slammed into her, hearing her moan as her body covetously tightened around me. "Damon."

I kissed her again as I took her over and over, slightly slower than the previous time, but still with need. I let her go, believing that she wouldn't push me away, and she pulled me closer to her. Elisa shocked me further by attempting to move me with her body, before she told me to roll over in a hoarse voice. I complied, taking her with me to watch as she rode my cock with her hands pressed to my chest. She was hot and tight, and I watched her rock against me for a long moment before I began to meet her thrust-for-thrust. Her nipples hardened as they bounced with the movement, and Elisa cried out as I leaned up to take one between my lips.

We came together, crying out as she closed her eyes and slowed her movements. It was just as intense as before, and I memorized her face as I shot deep inside of her for the second time. A fleeting image of her with my baby growing inside of her moved through my mind, but I pushed the idea away and felt her drop on top of me. I stroked her hair and listened to her uneven breathing as heat flowed between our bodies. "Do you even like your apartment? I think it's awful."

Elisa laughed slightly and pressed her lips to my shoulder. "I hate it. There's no privacy."

"It's not in a safe area," I added, as I felt her lips against my skin again.

"There are so many people living there in that small space," she told me, as I slipped my hands down to stroke her back.

"New employees get this place for six months, if they need it, not that Ken bothers to check the numbers. That's a good amount of time for you to see what happens, seeing as you graduate this year," I informed her, as she dropped her cheek against me.

"You're not going to let this go, are you?" Elisa asked, as I smiled.

"No, I'm not. I think this would benefit both of us." I closed my eyes and relaxed. "Not that I want there to be one, but there is room for a roommate here, if you choose one."

"If I could stay, I'd love to get my mother here. She lives in a terrible part of the city," Elisa admitted, as my curiosity was piqued. I asked her where and Elisa told me, making me wince. It was a step above the projects.

"Tell me about her," I urged her, as she kissed my chest.

"Dad left when I was five, and Mom had to take care of me all on her own. She worked so much, leaving me with Gram while she worked two, and sometimes three, jobs. When I was thirteen, Gram was gone, and I took care of myself mostly. I just watched her work so hard, just to keep a roof over my head and food on our table. I did my part by working hard at school to get into a good college, just to return the favor." She sighed. "The internship was a dream. I knew that I had a chance to make something of myself."

"That's why you're scared," I said, as she slid her hands under my arms.

"I could lose it all, along with my reputation. I won't be able to do anything for her." I pulled Elisa to me. "She's fifty-five and still working two jobs, just to keep her horrible apartment."

"I will do everything in my power to keep us secret, but I'm not letting you go. You'll move in here as soon as possible, and we'll keep that to ourselves, unless you spend time with anybody outside of the building," I was curious as much as I was concerned, and I waited for her answer.

"No, not anymore. I'll tell everyone that I live in the old apartment still, if they ask," Elisa murmured, as she trembled in my arms.

"I'll get an apartment cleaned up for your mom, too. She deserves to live somewhere safe." I planned on calling Ken as soon as possible and explaining the situation to him, even though it was so unlike me to do so. I couldn't figure out why I wanted to help Elisa so much. I just did. "It'll be okay, Elisa."

I asked if she was hungry and assured her that I'd order Thai food to be delivered. We dressed to go into the living room, and I showed her through the kitchen a bit and built a fire in the impressive fireplace that was just to the left of the television.

"This is so nice, Damon. I can't imagine how much it would cost per month."

"Don't worry about that. Most of it is for employees, and nobody will notice another couple of units being filled. All the residents are appreciative of the opportunity and quiet. You'll be safe here."

Elisa stared at me as she sat down on the couch beside me and pressed her lips together. I found something to watch on the television, and we snuggled together until the food came.

I asked about her scholarship, and just what it offered her, nodding when she explained that it covered full tuition, with a little extra. With the part time job with me, which I intended to keep going, she'd be okay. She even suggested that her mom live with her, but I wanted time to ourselves and the chance for Elisa to live on her own for a while. The money didn't matter. Her safety and happiness did.

I took her upstairs to the other bedroom, to show her how much bigger it was. I wanted her to stay in this room, because it seemed safer up here, even with the security system that I was going to have installed. Elisa walked around the spacious room, peeking into the attached master bathroom and the balcony that would offer an excellent view of the city. "It's lovely. I can imagine studying up here so peacefully, with the slider open when the weather is nice."

"I have other plans for this room," I told her, as she giggled and sat on the king-sized bed.

I could tell that she was tired from the emotions of the evening, as well as the sex we'd shared, and let her fall asleep beside me, with nothing more than a soft kiss. Regarding my lifestyle, the sex would be considered vanilla on many levels. In my soul, I knew that it was different, and that it had been so much more than a physical connection. I thought back to Sharon earlier that night and compared the experiences. Sharon was done with Elisa in my mind, and I knew that. Now that I'd felt what it was like to be inside of Elisa, I didn't want anyone else.

This was a problem. Elisa was my employee, and this was going against the rules set by me when I took over. I never planned on getting involved with anyone in my company, since I had plenty of women for that in my personal life. I was always strong at separating the two until I saw Elisa's face and felt the connection between us. It was something that I couldn't ignore, and I asked myself if I was willing to risk everything for her.

I finally slept beside her, something that was not normally part of my life. I always sent the woman away when I was finished and slept alone.

Everything was different now.

Elisa woke up late, since we'd left her purse with her phone in it downstairs. She panicked, since she was already late for classes. I calmed her down and made some coffee, assuring her that she was at the top of her class, and that one day wouldn't destroy that. It was disconcerting for me to see how obsessed Elisa was with doing what was expected of her, day in and day out. Elisa had been pressured from an early age, through no fault of her own, and I noted the slight circles under her eyes as she sipped coffee on the balcony. I wondered how Elisa viewed this offer of mine; as relief or just more pressure on her shoulders? Elisa was not used to people helping her, apart from her mother, and that was something that ultimately made her work twice as hard for anything that she wanted.

I could see that she was ready to jump out of her own skin, and I was willing to do anything to soothe her at this moment. I worked hard in a different way, without the pressure of finances. I understood that was a heavy load for someone that didn't have enough to make their life work.

I talked her into some late breakfast, sending Mark for some of the best bagels in the city and some more coffee. I loved Elisa's curvy little body, and I wanted to keep it that way. I didn't appreciate small women who worked out too much at a gym. I was all for being healthy, but I liked a little meat on women, as well, to add to the excitement in the bedroom. A bony ass was not fun to spank, but Elisa's was just full enough to grab and mark as I wanted to.

I watched her eat a muffin and drink more coffee, seemingly calmer and ready to tackle the rest of her day. She looked at me, and I saw the hesitation in her face. "I work with you today. Will that be awkward?"

"No, it will be better. You're an excellent employee, with or without this arrangement. Never think otherwise," I assured Elisa, as I checked the microwave and noted the time. I had blown off a lot of my own routine this morning, something that bothered me as I took my last sip of coffee. I'd make an excuse to everyone, even though I didn't need to be at work as early as I usually arrived. "I am going to head to my place to get ready for work. Are you okay here, or do you need Mark to get you home to change?"

"I brought clothes and things here for today, but thank you." Her smile was soft and beautiful, and I stepped forward to kiss her, my hands cupped around her face. "I don't think that thank you is enough to say, Damon. There's so much more, and I don't understand any of this, but thank you."

I kissed her again before heading home, showering quickly, and dressing for the office. I couldn't help but think back to the night and the incredible way that it made me feel. I was smiling when I stepped back into the car at my place, and Mark looked at me. "Is this serious?"

"Possibly," I replied, as he started the car. "I don't know what to make of it, Mark. That was never my style."

"Some things happen when they're meant to, Damon. This might be one of those times." I nodded at his words, as I leaned back against the seat and imagined Elisa in here with me.

26

ELISA

I took a shower in the huge marble space with three shower heads. Three! I'd never heard of such a thing before, but it felt so good. Somehow, there were products in there already, and I wondered if Damon had planned this ahead of time, wanting me to say yes. I loved the idea, but at the same time, it was too much. It wasn't something that I'd earned for myself, and I didn't take help easily, apart from my college scholarship.

Though I had worked for that, hadn't I? I sacrificed everything for that, things that normal high school students enjoy. Maybe this was when I would start to reap my rewards, though sleeping with my boss and taking an apartment from him was not one of my goals back then. I stepped out of the shower and dried myself off with the soft towels, looking over the counter and into mirror as I dried my hair. It was beautiful in here, and my bathroom at the other apartment would fit inside of this room. I wouldn't have to share it with anyone.

It just didn't feel right. Though this was just a two-bedroom apartment, it was so spacious. It was too big for just me, and I thought about having Mom move in with me, despite Damon's protests. Were we going to keep seeing one another outside of work, and that was why he protested? It would be awkward to be with him the way that I was last night with someone else home at night, since we clearly had incredible sexual chemistry.

What else was there, though?

I put on a little makeup to cover the circles under my eyes, then dressed in the black skirt and silk t-shirt that I'd brought along with me, frowning at the wrinkles that were in the red shirt, despite my careful packing of it. They weren't terrible, and it was Friday, a day that everyone dressed casually, unless they had a meeting. This would be considered dressy, but I liked wearing feminine clothes to work, and I loved that Damon wore suits every day. I blushed at the idea of seeing him again today when I went to his office. Last night was my first time enjoying sex without inhibitions, and I had shocked myself the second time, when I took control. I could tell that he preferred to have control, and my mind wandered to how hard he liked to go. I read books and heard girls talk at school, and it seemed to be a thing. I didn't understand it all completely, but I could ask him. I blushed. How embarrassing.

I left the apartment with my backpack slung over my shoulders and looked around carefully at my surroundings during the day. It was quiet and safe to assume that most of these people worked days here. I went to the main street and started to walk towards the office. It was only a couple of blocks away, and I could see this being very convenient for someone who worked for Elkus Manfredi and had just moved or who didn't have a car, like me. The walk was pleasant, and, at night, it wouldn't be too terrible. I wanted to keep the apartment, badly. It would help me so much with school, and I could study productively from home instead going to a noisy coffee shop and spending money I didn't have. That was my option when I didn't want to take a car back to school to use the library if I'd already been home, but neither option was pleasant. I thought of what else I could do alone and blushed as I walked through the glass doors.

I joined my team for the first part of the day, feeling inspired and adding a lot to the current project as Autumn smiled at me. She was the most supportive, besides Vince, and seemed to have dropped the subject of Damon. I'd never let her find out about us. I smiled back, thankful for her notice of my enthusiasm.

We headed out to lunch as a group, all excited about what was coming together as we headed to the deli down the street. Devin was just walking inside, and I looked forward in concern, as I wondered if there would be any confrontation once we interacted. Autumn called his name as she opened the door to go inside and he glanced up, letting his gaze pass over the group of us. There was no change in expression when he saw me, and I let out a sigh of relief. "Join us?" He called out, and Autumn nodded as I forced a small smile on my face.

We grabbed a big table in the back, and I sat across the table from Devin as he asked Autumn how our project was going. Everyone went back and forth, discussing things as I ate slowly and paid attention. I noticed that Devin looked at me a few times, but not in the way I'd expected after I turned him down at his apartment that night.

It wasn't anger that he showed me, but more disappointment. We'd kissed for a while on his couch, and, once I knew that it was headed further, I had pulled away. Damon was too much on my mind to do anything else with Devin, especially seeing him on the street just hours before. I explained that I wasn't ready for anything serious yet, since I was busy with school and the internship. Devin was disappointed, but he claimed that he understood before kissing me softly and taking me home. I wasn't in the position to tell anyone no very often, and it was uncomfortable.

I noticed that he didn't try to contact me after that, especially as I'd lied about seeing someone at school. I was young, and that's how other people my age seemed to behave,, so I didn't think it should seem odd. He was a great looking guy who could date anyone he wanted to, but I could still see feelings in Devin's eyes as they met mine when we were finishing lunch. He joined me on the sidewalk as we left, and I clutched my purse to my side and tried to act natural. "How are you doing?" His voice was casual, and I smiled in his direction.

"I love the job. The team is fantastic," I replied, as I glanced up in their direction.

"Yeah. Autumn has nice things to say about you." Devin let his eyes rest on her for a moment, and I wondered if there was something between them. She had a long-term boyfriend, from what I'd heard, but we weren't close friends. "I heard you're seeing a guy at school."

"I'm sorry. The timing was just wrong. It was unexpected, and it's so casual, since the circumstances are still the same," I told Devin, as I looked forward. The circumstances were nothing like before now, and it was a new game.

"Is he good to you?" Devin asked in a gruff voice, as I looked at him.

"I guess so, sure. It's new." He nodded and looked forward.

"You deserve that."

I thanked him as we walked into the building and made our way to the elevators. I looked over to see Damon speaking with a beautiful woman by the main desk, an older one who seemed charmed by whatever he was telling her. I forced my eyes away, remembering who I was with, and led the way into the spacious elevator car as my body ached for him. It was painful, and I told the others that I'd see them in a bit as they got off on floor five.

"Where are you going?" Devin asked, as he looked curiously at me before glancing at the buttons.

"She's helping the big boss a few days a week," Autumn said, as the door closed too quickly to see anyone's reaction. I dropped against the wall and took a deep breath as the elevator kept going up, praying that my face had been neutral during the last few minutes. I couldn't blow this. My body heated up, and I let myself wonder who the woman talking to Damon was. I knew that sleeping with Damon would increase my feelings for him, and perhaps a small part of me wished that I'd stopped it, but it was minute if I looked at the big picture. I was just scared, and that was normal.

I managed to regain my composure as I reached my floor, raising my head high as I made my way to his office and saw the closed door.

I tapped on it and unlocked the door when there was no reply, letting myself in and looking around as I set my purse down on the couch. My eyes lingered on the new shoes that matched my outfit for a long moment.

I pulled my iPad out of the bag and walked over to the desk to let it warm up. My work phone was always on, but it was silent today, making me wonder if Damon regretted the night before. I felt torn between being a girl and a woman with these crazy thoughts, and I tried to reason with myself. He was generous with me and concerned for my well-being. That was a good sign. Leave it at that and stop obsessing.

The door opened, and I jumped before I glanced up and saw Damon coming through with a cold look in his eyes. "Damon?" I asked, as I frowned and tried to think of what I'd done. He hadn't even see me earlier in the lobby, or had he? Devin.

"What was that, earlier in the lobby?" He asked point blank, as he stalked across the room towards me.

"I think I could ask the same thing. Who was the woman, Damon?" I shot back, as my jealousy poured out of me and onto the floor in a pile of shame. I felt my cheeks flush, and he raised an eyebrow at me.

"Jesus fucking Christ. You sound like a jealous teenager," he told me, as I stared at him.

"I practically am. I'm still in college, Damon." He stopped in front of me, eyes flashing as he gripped my face, looking into my eyes.

"Don't remind me. You didn't seem like one last night when you were riding me," he said, as I struggled in his grip. "I like that confident, wanting side of you. Where is it right now, Elisa?" His voice was demanding, as I felt my knees trembling as I sat on the desk.

"You overwhelm me, Damon. You confuse me," I told him, as he slipped a hand behind my neck and kissed me. I moaned against him, not finished arguing as my body gave in to my need for him. My skirt was pushed up, and he ripped my panties down, plunging his fingers inside of me as his tongue circled mine. I whimpered as he pressed in deeper and harder, ready to burst before he told me to wait.

"Hold it. I'll tell you when," Damon said to me, as my eyes widened and I tried to shut off the sensations flowing through my body. How was I supposed to not come when he was dragging his fingers against the walls of my pussy, finding every sensitive spot that I had?

"How?" I groaned, as I stayed still and tried to ignore everything that was happening to me.

"Willpower," Damon told me, as he manipulated my body and pressed his lips against my neck. It seemed like hours, but was probably more like minutes before he started thumbing my clit and whispered for me to let go.

"Fuck," I cried out, as my body exploded and I jerked against him. "What was that?"

"That was control," Damon told me, as he pulled away to kiss my lips. "I'll get you some water from the fridge."

I dropped back onto the desk as I sucked my breath in and let my body recover. That was so intense that I had almost forgotten about being jealous, at least until I saw Damon walk back into the room with water. My eyes were dazed as I stared at him, and he looked back at me. I took the water from him and downed half of it as I closed my eyes.

"The woman was a friend of my mother's. I hadn't seen her in a couple of years, and she wanted to take me to lunch."

"Oh," I felt stupid and slid down from the desk to sit in a seat as I looked around the floor for my underwear, if they had even survived. They were near my feet, and I blinked at them for a moment. "I'm sorry."

"Explain why you were with Devin," he suggested, as I let out a sigh.

"It was nothing. I was with my group, and Devin was with his at the deli. Autumn knows him, so we shared a table. I barely spoke to him on my own, and, when we did, I assured him that I was with someone," I told him, as he looked at me carefully. "I swear. Do you think I could want anyone else after last night?"

"I'd hope not. I know that I don't," Damon said, as if it surprised him. Confusion flooded me again. "Maybe we'll have to work on your control from now on."

I had no idea how I was supposed to work after that. Somehow, I made it through the day and went to dinner with Damon. I couldn't help but glance around the lobby as we left together. It was empty, and I followed him to his car as I kept my eyes forward and my hands at my side. We'd touched behind his closed door and we would again, later, but not here. Not in public. Mark opened the car door for me with a smile as I nodded at him and slipped into the car with Damon following me. "Where are we going?" I asked, as he smiled mysteriously.

"You'll see," Damon told me as he pulled me to his side to kiss me. I allowed him his moment as we drove through the streets, wrapped up together. It felt good in his arms, and I noticed that the car stopped before I looked out of the windows. We were at L'ESPALIER, one of the finest restaurants in the area, and I smiled at him.

We got out, and he led me inside as he told the beautiful hostess that he had a reservation. The woman nodded as she gazed at him with wide eyes before glancing at me with a small smile. The woman led us to a table located in the kitchen, where the chefs were in action, and I laughed as we sat down. "This is different."

27

DAMON

In between watching the preparation and tasting the variety of dishes that we sampled, Elisa accepted my offer of the apartment and told me that she'd tell her roommates in the next day or two. She was going to do the right thing and pay them for the next month in rent, so it wouldn't put the other students in a bind, which I admired. Elisa was kind and thoughtful. She was someone who I knew would care for me the way I wanted a woman to, if I was serious about anyone. I asked her how much she needed to move, and she laughed when she explained that the apartment was fully furnished as well, just with a much lower-grade selection than I was giving her.

"I was thinking, though, and I feel guilty that you're holding a whole other unit for Mom. She can stay with me, since it's so big. I don't think that she'll quit both jobs after the move, but I'm hoping to convince her to drop one and go part-time at the other one," Elisa said, as she looked shyly at me. "We'll have privacy, if that's what you want. I mean, if you'll be staying there with me sometimes."

"You've assumed correctly, Elisa. I don't just offer this to any woman," I reminded her, as another dish was brought around. This was a chicken dish, consisting of tender meat and crispy skin, and I watched as Elisa moaned as she tasted it.

We left after a lot of good food and some wine, and Mark opened the door to the car for us as Elisa giggled. "Does he have a life apart from this?" She asked, once inside the car, with a wave if her hand.

"He'll be taking the car home, once he drops us off at my place," I replied, as she looked at me.

"Not the apartment?"

"I thought I'd show you my home," I told her, as she smiled and sat back against the leather.

"Thank you for dinner. That was a great night," she said, as she kissed my neck.

Mark took my private entrance, pulling into the garage and dipping low to drive us to the elevator. He let us out and bid us both good night, as he gave us a warm smile. I led Elisa to door by the hand, and she waved to Mark before wrapping an arm around my waist.

I heard heels clicking in the garage and turned my head to see Natalie looking back at me as she walked towards her car. She didn't have a penthouse like I did, so I was surprised and concerned that it blew my anonymity. "Do you know her?" Elisa asked in a loud whisper, as Natalie narrowed her eyes at me.

"Just another resident in the building," I assured Elisa, before turning towards the open door.

We went up to my place and walked inside as I locked the door and she stopped walking just to look around. "This is..."

"I call it home," I said, as I slipped her jacket off to hang by the door.

"Incredible," she breathed, as she stepped forward and walked over to the windows to look over the city. I knew that I had an elegant apartment, since I had custom ordered everything in it, but it was nice to see the childlike joy on her face. "I never lived anywhere close to this. I guess you probably did."

"We were always comfortable, Elisa. This is more my own, though," I walked over and started a fire, while she looked outside for a few more moments.

"How many bedrooms does this have?" I heard her ask as I stoked the fire with the tools that I kept nearby, frowning at the ash collecting at the end of the shiny brass.

"Four. Most of the space is this room and the kitchen, though the master bedroom is large," I replied, as she sat down behind me. "I use the other rooms for an office, a spare room, and then another, more personalized extra room."

"Personalized?" She asked, with another one of her goddamn giggles, as I stood and ran my hands down my pants. I had slipped the coat and suit jacket off upon arriving home, and I turned to stare at her as I loosened my tie. Her eyes were dark and hungry as she leaned forward on the couch and licked her lips.

"Did you like holding it earlier today?" I watched her face flush as she thought about my question, making me hard as I left my tie loose around my neck. I remembered the look in her eyes the previous time that I did that, and I had plans with it.

"I did," she told me, as a naughty look crossed her face. I wanted to see a lot more of it, and I walked over to her before dropping on the couch beside her. "Why? Do you want to do that again?"

"Yes," she whispered, as her green eyes caught mine with an intense look. I wondered how far to take it tonight as I leaned in to kiss her, first slowly and then with a heat that filled the room as we both deepened it.

There was my bedroom or the other room. Was it too much yet? I knew that Elisa had expressed a previous concern about my past, and she might not feel that way once she saw what it held. I didn't use my home often for sex, but there were the precious few women who had become more to me. That was when I designed the other room.

Nobody meant what Elisa did to me, and had never even come close. I kissed her harder, testing her desire as she slipped her hand down between my legs and squeezed. "I want to show you something, Elisa."

"What?" She asked breathlessly, before she kissed me again. The kiss lasted a few minutes as she moved onto my lap and distracted me from my plan, my hands moving to cup her ass. I wanted to rip off all her clothes and fuck her right here, but I focused and pulled away.

"Come with me," I told her, as I pushed her off of me gently and went to get some water. We were going to need it. I held the bottles of water as I led Elisa down the long hallway and unlocked the door with the key that I pulled from the drawer in the kitchen. I paused before I took her hand and brought her inside, watching as her mouth dropped open and her eyes widen.

THE INTERN INSTALLMENT BOOK 5

An Alpha Billionaire Romance

By Michelle Love

ELISA

He took me into another room that was lit by a large glass chandelier hanging from the ceiling. It was another bedroom, but more. It looked like sin, with the prominent iron headboard that offered several areas to be tied to, with a little something at the foot of the bed as well. I could see all the shelving and cabinets and I felt my thighs heat up as I wondered what was in there. I felt Damon slide his hands over my hips, making me jump at the heat that I felt from his hands. "I can do incredible things to your body in here," he promised me, as I licked my lips.

"So I see," I replied, as I let the jealousy in my heart wind around my body. I reminded myself that he had arranged an apartment for me, as well as my mother. I knew that he cared for me, no matter what his past might include. I had to let that go. I had to see where this would go. "What do you want me to do in here?"

"I'd like to start slowly. First, I want to tie you up and work on the control we previously discussed. I'd have complete control of the situation, and I'd like to feel out your limits," Damon told me, as I shivered. "The bed is custom made for various kinds of restraint."

"I guessed as much. It's beautiful," I told him, as Damon chuckled darkly.

"I don't know if I'd refer to it like that," he said, as I turned slowly in his arms. "This isn't vanilla in here, Elisa. This can get rough."

"You wouldn't hurt me. You wouldn't push me if I asked you to stop," I told Damon, as his eyes burned brightly in the light.

"I wouldn't do that," Damon told me, as I smiled and stood on my toes to kiss him.

"Why do I think this is more than that?" I whispered, before his lips caught mine in a heated kiss. I wrapped my arms around his neck and he lifted me, carrying me across the large room to the bed as our tongues danced together. I felt the heat thick in my veins as I pulled him closer, inviting him to do what he wanted. I knew what this room was, at least in part, and I felt ready for it.

I wanted to hold onto Damon, and taking a step into his world was going to be necessary for that to happen. It might excite my otherwise dull life as well.

I stripped off my clothes when Damon ordered me to in a soft voice with a firm tone. I was shaking as I dropped them onto the floor and turned my gaze to him, seeing his eyes hungry as they took me in. He strode to one of the cabinets, removing some rope from it and turning it in his hand.

"Get on your back and spread your arms and legs," Damon told me, as I complied, blushing at the way I was exposed. Damon focused on the knots, keeping them comfortable and allowing me enough room to move around. I knew that I couldn't touch him, though, and the idea bothered me and excited me all at once. I saw him slide his eyes up my legs to take in my glistening pussy as he secured my feet, taking away any control from me as I trembled.

I was quiet as he stripped, proudly displaying his muscled planes and stunning body before he sat down on the bed between my legs. "We'll start slow, Elisa. I want to make you enjoy this, but if you don't, just tell me to slow down. I don't want to scare you, and doing it this way is testing my control."

"Okay," I said, as he nodded and looked over my body slowly. My nipples were hard and achy while I felt my core growing wetter with the intensity of his eyes. It was almost too much, and I struggled against the binds as he rested a hand on my calf. The slight touch made me jump, and he stroked my skin as he told me to calm down and that I was safe. Damon took something in his hand and dimmed the lights a bit, creating a calm sensation in me as he stroked my leg, his hand rising higher and higher. The combination of desire and contentment was overwhelming to me, and I jerked as he slipped his fingers over my pussy.

"So wet for me," he murmured, as he stroked my clit, smiling at my low moan. "This is your spot, Elisa. This is your center." I nodded, as he moved his hand slowly over me, just teasing my swollen nub. One finger slid inside of me, stroking my inner walls firmly as I squirmed and bit my lip. I never knew my own sensitivity before Damon, and it was killing me that I wasn't going to be able to come soon. I wanted that. I wanted to coat his fingers and scream his name in this room, followed by begging him to fuck me hard. I was ready, but I suspected that he knew that.

"Damon," I cried out, as he found a place that made me nearly explode before moving away from it with a smile on his face. "That's not fair. It felt so good."

"I know," he teased me, as I lowered my gaze to meet his eyes as he stroked my slick inner thighs that I knew had to be pooling onto the bed by now. We stared at one another for a long moment as he seemed to consider his next move, looking dangerous and sexy as sin.

He moved to sit beside me, his eyes circling my nipples as they seemed to reach to him. "Fuck, they ache," I said, as he reached out and smoothed his hand over the skin just underneath my breasts. His finger slid up, stroking the right one as I closed my eyes and memorized the feeling. I could come from this in my unsettled state, but I was aware that he knew that and would prevent it. "How can you stand this?"

"I am hard as a rock right now, Elisa. It's not easy, but we need this step," his voice was low, and I could hear him controlling it as he plucked at me, causing me to jerk again. "When I do fuck you, you are going to be wet with all the orgasms that I allowed you, tight for my cock."

"Oh, God," I moaned, as he lowered his mouth to kiss my stomach, moving slowly up to take one of my nipples into his mouth. Damon used his mouth on me, drawing me close to an orgasm before he pulled away. Slowly, he added light clips to my nipples and teased my clit with a dildo with the vibration on low, pulling away every time I got close. I was hoarse when he finally slipped two fingers inside of me, stroking me hard as I rocked with him.

"Come, Elisa," he whispered in my ear, as I screamed. My body rocked forward, every nerve ending in my body feeling this orgasm. It was worth the torture in that moment, even though it felt like hours' worth of it. I whimpered at the end as he stroked me slowly, prolonging the pleasure. "How did that feel?"

"Amazing," I panted, as I closed my eyes and took a few deep breaths. Every muscle ached with it, and I felt him move from the bed, returning quickly. Something was placed against my mouth, and I cracked one eye to see a bottle of water in Damon's hand. I sucked and found it to be the kind of lid that I could control. I drank gratefully from it.

When I was rested, he moved between my legs and teased my pussy with his mouth. Damon cleaned me from the previous orgasm, drawing me closer to another before he'd pull away and nibble on the soft skin of my inner thigh. I played back the previous one in my head, telling myself that it was worth it as he dragged my clit between his teeth and made me moan. I was closer to having him inside of me, fucking me raw as I begged him for more.

Damon was taking away all of my will power as he pleasured me to the edge, pulling away too many times. I cried out with it, begging him, then telling him that I hated him. When he finally told me to let go and took me between his teeth again, I screamed and flooded his lips. Damon drank me in, stroking my clit with his thumb as I felt my body go through the intense process all over again.

I opened my eyes as he released my feet and told me to get on my knees. "I love how tight a woman is after I've tasted her," he said, as I tried to find the strength to move. It was too much, and I groaned as I flipped over, moving to my knees. I suddenly found something inside of me as I heard the tearing of a wrapper, then felt Damon drive himself inside of me. I knew how much everything had gotten to him as he moved rough and fast, and I rocked with him. I was soaked with need and needed this. He slapped my ass as he pulled back, making me cry out.

Damon came with a roar, gripping my hips as he filled the condom, and I came for the third time that night. I didn't know how long we'd been in here, but it felt like days at that point. He moved away from me on shaking legs and grabbed the water, offering it to me before he took a long sip. "It was so hard not to just shove you on your stomach and do that in the beginning. Was it worth the wait?" Damon asked me, as I considered my answer for a few moments, in part because I was having trouble breathing.

"Yes," I replied in a hoarse whisper, as I felt him kiss my shoulder before untying the ropes.

He rested for a few moments before lifting me into his arms and carrying me to another room. It was a bedroom, as big as the other, but more like a master bedroom. It had a huge bed, a fireplace that took up the entire wall, and a big screen television on the wall that we were facing. I felt him set me on that bed, naked and probably a hot mess, and looked into his eyes by the light of the lamp in the corner of the room. "I prefer to sleep in here."

"I'm staying?" I asked, as he nodded.

"You might never leave at this point," Damon assured me, as he pulled down the comforter and sheets before lifting me and setting me near the pillows.

"I'm a mess, Damon," I told him as he licked his lips. "I can wash the sheets tonight if you want."

No, I want your scent on them and in my room. I want to be reminded of everything that just happened," Damon told me, before he kissed me. "I want to feel you around me again in here, slower. More intimately."

"I'd like that," I told him, as he moved beside me to kiss me slowly. It was passionate, but didn't feel rushed. It felt perfect. I wanted to please him to show him my gratitude for the events in the other room, and Damon allowed me to push him to the mattress and crawl down his body to his cock. I wanted to taste him now.

He held my hair as I bobbed over him, my mouth tight and greedy. Damon gave me control now, groaning as I increased the pace and beginning to rock with me. He came with a grunt, filling my mouth and throat, as if he knew that's what I wanted.

It was.

He had to pull me from him as I tried to swallow every last bit of his essence. "What have I done to you?" Damon mused, as he took in the wild look in my eyes with a soft gaze. "I am turning you into a monster."

It wasn't long before he was hard again and we were pressed together, him above me as he slid in and out of me. It was slow and bordering on sweet as I held him close and wrapped my legs around him. Damon's mouth drifted down to my nipples, my neck, and my lips, even though I was previously filled with him. He didn't seem to care, making me wonder about him.

I came a moment before he did, feeling his lips in my hair as he jerked above me. I was overwhelmed, wondering what I'd ever go back to when this ended.

30

DAMON

E lisa fell asleep before I did, curled up in a heap after everything I'd put her through. I watched her as I allowed myself to relax, covering her with the blankets and stroking her hair back. She was innocent before me, but so open to my ideas, and I craved her again as I took in her beautiful face. I knew that she was perfect. The unpleasant idea of my preparing her for another man crossed my mind, and I slipped under the covers with a frown.

We had a lot stacked against us, Elisa and me. There was the fact that I was her boss and this was against company policy, to begin with. There was the chance of gossip, which could be cruel and heartless, hurting her in the end. There was my past, which could threaten us at any time and possibly frighten her off.

I could give her the world if she wanted it. I had already given her an apartment for her and her mother, but I sensed that Elisa wouldn't want to stay home while I covered the rent and every other expense in her life. She had too much pride and had worked hard to rise above her life for so long now that it was in her blood.

I could count the women who begged me for just that on two hands. Why was I falling for the stubborn one?

I settled close to her body, sliding my arm around her as I drifted off to sleep. It was Friday night, and we could sleep in tomorrow, maybe even leave the city and spend the day together. I could stay in bed with her and be happy, but Elisa deserved to live after all her hard work. I wanted to show her the other side of life.'

When I woke up in the morning, I could see the fog thick in the air through my wall of windows. Elisa was pressed against me, hot and bare, and I felt my body react to her skin. I wanted to take her quietly, slipping inside of her as she opened her eyes, but I moved slowly between her legs and spread them as she moaned in her sleep. I slid down to her pussy, still covered in her juices from the night before. I liked a dirty girl in the morning, and I pressed my mouth over her and licked slowly with my tongue.

"What?" Elisa moaned, as she moved against me and I raised my eyes to see her staring at me. "I was afraid that it was all a dream." I continued to lick her, separating her to find her clit hard for me as I stroked it firmly. "Damon, you feel so good." I licked and sucked, even using my teeth as she just watched me.

Without my urging, Elisa held onto her release with her eyes wide and bright before she cried out and jerked against me. "The student learns," I noted, as she looked at me with a big smile. Elisa looked beautiful with her cheeks flushed and glowing as she reached down to pull me up towards her.

"She does. Get up here and reward me," she mumbled, before claiming my lips in a kiss, tasting herself on them as she kissed me slowly and hungrily. I reached for one of the condoms on the night stand beside the bed and managed to get it on one-handed as she held me close. I heard her giggling as I dropped between her legs and eased the head of my cock inside of her, causing the giggles to turn to moans. We moved together, slow and hard, both of us needing the other to give us the release that we craved.

I knew that I was addicted to this woman as I came crying out her name, and I fought the nagging thoughts telling me that it wouldn't work out. It was difficult, but I'd make it work somehow. "How would you feel about going to the coast today?" I asked her, as she looked across the room through the windows.

"It looks pretty cold to me," Elisa replied warily, as I smiled. "I don't have any clothes, except the ones I brought here."

"We'll get you something, hit a diner on the way for breakfast and just drive. I want to get out of the city." I looked at her, as she smiled and nodded. "Shower with me?"

That took some time, since things heated up under the water and I was soon inside of her, pressing her against the blue tiled wall as she wrapped her body around mine. Elisa dried her hair with a towel and pulled something out of her purse before she ran a comb through her hair.

"Frizz," she said simply, as I watched her, not used to a woman being around in this way. They were usually gone after the condom was off. Not too many women saw this side of my life, or even my bedroom. She pulled her hair up on the top of her head and asked me if I had a toothbrush, tilting her head as I produced a new one in the package. "I hope that you don't have a lot of those."

"I buy a few at a time, so I don't run out. They don't get used by anybody but myself, and now you, unless a friend or family visits." I stepped out of the bathroom to dry off, sensing that she was uncomfortable. Everything this morning had been extremely intimate, which was something that Elisa wasn't accustomed to. I needed to allow her space, as well as myself, and I strode to the closet to find clothes for the day. I selected some jeans and a dark grey Henley that I planned to cover with a thick jacket. This trip was not about a walk on the beach, but more about the drive and just getting away. There were some fabulous restaurants to eat at, as well, and shops that I thought Elisa might love.

I finished with boots as Elisa stepped out of the bathroom, wearing the clothes from the day before. The best part was that I knew her underwear were ruined from the night before, but I pushed that thought away and pulled an extra jacket from the closet for her.

I took her to my Range Rover and opened the door before starting the engine and pulling out onto the main road. We stopped at a department store, and she balked at the name before grudgingly allowing me to buy her some jeans, a thermal, a Henley to wear over that, and some sturdy boots that would keep her feet warm. "You do too much for me," Elisa told me, as we stopped by a bathroom so she could change into her new clothes.

"I like that, Elisa. I like that I'm able to," I reminded her, as we went back to the car together. We got out of town, and I found a hole-in-the-wall diner on the freeway when we both felt hungry. We sipped strong coffee and ate greasy bacon and eggs as I watched her carefully. I asked her what she liked to do on a road trip, making her giggle as she admitted to not having been on too many in her life. That led to her asking about the places I had been, and I felt guilty when I responded that I'd traveled the world. I hoped to someday show her the best places.

We hit the road again, driving towards Cape Cod. I knew that there was enough there to keep us busy there, bad weather or not, and I watched as she seemed to let go of the chip on her shoulder from breakfast. Elisa was beautiful when she smiled. She needed to relax more. We got closer, and she stared out of the windows at the ocean and sandy beaches, hopeful since the sun was coming out through the fog. "Maybe we can walk a little bit?" She asked, as I grinned and nodded.

I parked, and we got out and strolled along the sand. The waves were strong and the wind was cold as she pulled my jacket closer around her body. "What do you think?" I asked, stopping her so I could zip her up and looked her over. "I should have bought us hats. I didn't even think of it."

"You don't date, right? Typically, I mean?" Her question came from nowhere, and I looked at her for a moment before nodding. "Why not? You're great at this...all of this."

"I don't know. I've avoided it for so long and focused on work, but...this is comfortable. I think it's you more than it is the situation." I turned to stare at the sea for a moment as confusion swirled through my brain. I knew that this was moving at the speed of light with the apartment and spending the night together, and I tried to make sense of it. I'd been all over the world, never wanting the company of a woman, unless it was just for a night for a quick fuck. I had party girls over the years, as well, but I never let my walls down with them like I was with Elisa. There was just something about her.

"I think you're great. I have no idea why you're with me, but I'll take it," She said, as I looked in her face. "I don't know what I'm doing either, but we can figure it out together."

I took her hand and led her down the beach after we shared a long kiss, talking about some of the other beaches in the area and further away that I loved. I pointed towards the shops and restaurants in the distance, and she smiled as she looked all around, reminding me of a child on Christmas morning.

That thought sat in my stomach in a knot. I'd never considered marriage or kids before. I was all about work, but things were shifting now, and I was unable to stop that. The problem was that, to keep Elisa, I'd have to rip her dreams of a good job and future for herself away to do so. I didn't want to take away her fierce independence, but I also knew that she wouldn't want to be taken care of. There had to be a compromise, and I had no idea what it was, other than hiding this during the week. I didn't think I could do that for too long after being here with Elisa in the open air, holding hands and laughing.

We spent hours on the beach, collecting a few shells, until we were both freezing. I opened the car door for her and got everything warmed up as we headed somewhere for some hot coffee, listening to Elisa's teeth chattering as she sat beside me. "Isn't it warming up enough?" I asked impatiently, knowing how many bells and whistles this vehicle offered.

"I think it's the difference in temperature, Damon. I'll be okay."

I smiled at her as I found a drive through coffee shop, ordering two coffees and parking with the car running to keep us warm. We sipped the drinks and looked at the late afternoon sky as the clouds began to roll in again.

"Want to look at some of the shops?" I asked, as she finished her coffee and nodded. We'd been sitting for a while and didn't have a lot of time left. I drove to park in the middle of everything and let her lead the way, learning about her love for art, even though she didn't think that she could paint. I learned that she had collected moons since she was little girl, and that her grandmother had taught her to wish on the one in the sky at night, instead of the stars. Elise was a very animated girl when she let her walls down, and she led me from shop to shop as I tried to remember what she liked the best in each one.

She insisted on buying a few things with her own money, holding onto the small bags with a big smile before she hugged me. "I couldn't do this without you, Damon. You've helped me so much." Elisa looked around slowly before she kissed me, and I heard the whispers across the room of the wealthy women who had been eying me for most of the afternoon. "Thank you. I'll be eternally grateful."

I looked like I belonged with the other women in my clothes, some of the most expensive items that money could buy. That had been a part of my entire life, but in this moment, I thought that I could give it all up for an average life like this. Even Elisa was dressed in fine clothes right now, thanks to our stop, but she looked young and beautiful with her clean face and smile. She would never fit into that world. "It's a pleasure to see you smile, Elisa," I assured her, as she blushed and looked away. We left that shop and I didn't even acknowledge the women with a look as I led her out of the door.

They'd never hold a candle to her.

31

ELISA

T he day was magical. I finally admitted to being hungry and watched as Damon led me to a beautiful restaurant that probably had a beautiful view of the water during the day. It was a seafood place that was very classy and elegant. I felt under-dressed as we walked to the table, following the hostess, but Damon walked with his head high and confidence oozing from his pores. The table was round and intimate, set by the window and a beautiful fire-place, and Damon ordered wine immediately as someone arrived to take our drink order.

I didn't eat in places like this. For Mom and me, Red Robin was a treat, and this was beyond my wildest dreams. When I thought about the night as a whole; the room and being here, it seemed surreal. I never thought I'd be the kind of woman to enjoy that with a man. I never thought I'd be the kind of woman to sit here and enjoy a fine meal with a man that looked like Damon, and I wasn't sure I'd ever be confident in that role.

I didn't think I was the kind of woman to keep him.

The wine arrived, and there was a process to the drinking it. I sipped it once Damon seemed to have approved the selection, gazing at him across the table while I searched the menu. I loved seafood, but wasn't too familiar with it, and I asked Damon what was good. He suggested shrimp or crab, since it had a few options of how it was cooked, and I blushed as I selected a platter that offered both. There was no price on the menu, and I assumed that meant it was expensive as I tried to fight the urge to add everything up in my mind. Damon had money that he was willing to spend, and I needed to feel comfortable with that fact.

The food was amazing, even as I struggled with cracking the crab legs. It was well worth it as I pulled the meat out and enjoyed the light, sweet taste. "This is delicious," I told Damon, as he smiled calmly at me. He offered me a bite of his steak and it melted in my mouth, leaving me moaning while his eyes darkened. The shrimp was cooked in butter and garlic and quite strong, but good as well. They offered bread in a tray, and I ate it eagerly in between sips of wine.

I leaned back as I set my fork down, full and sleepy. The sky was bright with stars and a sliver of a moon as I looked over the ocean. I wanted to stay the night and wake up here with Damon, and I nibbled on my lip as I considered asking him about the idea. I could wear the same clothes tomorrow since they were so new.

Tomorrow.

What would we do tomorrow? Would he drop me home, and that would be it? I knew that I had to tell my roommates that I was moving out, since I'd accepted the apartment, but I didn't want it without Damon. I felt so selfish as we walked to the car and he opened the door.

"Have you ever stayed here?" I asked softly, as he started to close the door.

"A few times. It's a great place to spend the weekend," Damon replied, as he leaned into the car. "Did you want to?"

"We don't have clothes, or anything at all. We don't have to," I said, counting the money in my bank account as I decided what I could afford.

"We'll sleep naked, so clothes aren't an issue. We can wear these on the way home tomorrow and stop at the store for anything you need for the bathroom. There's a great bed and breakfast with an amazing view of the sunrise in the morning. We can see if they have any free rooms. It won't be a long stay, but we can make the best of it." Damon walked around and got in the car before he finished his thoughts and reached for his phone in his jacket. He dialed and greeted the person at the other end, securing us a room and starting the engine.

We did stop and get some products, so I could look human in the morning, before we drove to the inn, called the Lamb and Lion. Damon explained that it was a mix of bed and breakfast and hotel. He wished that we could stay longer to enjoy all the perks that they offered.

He checked in and led us to a room around the building. I gasped when I saw it. There was a fireplace, a claw tooth tub, a big bathroom, and a gorgeous bed. It was beautiful. I walked to the window, even though it was dark, and could make out the waves in the dim light as I smiled. It was going to be amazing tomorrow. "How much is it to split the room?" I asked, as I turned back to smile at Damon.

"Split the room?" He asked, as he walked towards me. "You have an extra month of rent to pay, Elisa. I've got this."

"Will you always?" I asked, as I stared at him.

"Let's take a bath and relax. I'll start a fire," Damon suggested, as pain crossed his face. He went to get some logs from the balcony and lit a crackling fire while I ran the hot water for the bath, adding a little of the lavender bubbles from the counter. I didn't know how much he'd want, so I kept it light, enjoying the scent in the air. "I wish they made that in the scent that you wear. I'm addicted to it." I turned to look at Damon as he smiled at me. "This isn't a competition, Elisa. I like spoiling you."

"I just want to help, I think. I am not used to being taken care of."

"Let's get you settled in your new apartment, and we'll go from there," Damon said gently, as he pulled the jacket from my shoulders. "For now, let's relax in style." He stripped me of my clothing, folding it, and placing it somewhere in the room before he walked back in naked. I blushed as he slid into the hot water, sighing happily. "Get in."

I stepped in and moved into the water, feeling his eyes rake over me. Once settled, I leaned back against him as Damon kissed my neck, telling me how beautiful I was. "Thank you," I replied, as I closed my eyes and let my body relax. "What are we going to do Monday?" I asked him in the dim light of the candles that I'd lit before turning off the lights.

"We are going to work and keep this between us. I can't say that it will be easy, but for now, it's the only choice. I want to keep seeing you, Elisa." I smiled as the steam and scents filled my nose. "I want you to let me spoil you."

"I know. I'm trying," I admitted as his hands slid down my body. "I have been on my own for so long, Damon. I'm scared to get too comfortable, and the fact that we work together...it scares me."

"I'll keep this between us so nobody will know in the building. I prefer to keep my private life under wraps to begin with. We can stay at my apartment at night and just stay in. Perhaps I can get you a job at another location, or with a colleague, where we can be together out in the open. I know a lot of people."

A tear slid down my cheek. I had my dream job right now, earning it with my hard work. Damon had told me how he had tried to talk everyone out of hiring me, but they'd insisted. I didn't want a job as a favor to Damon, and, at this moment, I didn't even want the apartment. Love had never been an option for me, and, as much as I thought I was falling for Damon, I didn't want to give up my dream for him. Not yet. "Maybe I can just work with my team from now on and keep my distance. We can say that you didn't need me anymore, or something."

"Are you pulling away from me?" Damon asked.

I shook my head slowly. "It's a thought, Damon. It would draw less attention to us."

"I don't want to not see you at the office. It's the best part of my day," Damon told me, as I smiled weakly.

"We'll have time to see each other after work. I just feel like I need some space from everyone's prying eyes. I don't know," I babbled, as he pulled me close to him.

"Stop this, Elisa. Relax," I heard pain in his voice as he stroked my arms and tried to calm me down.

I shut up and tried to let the hot water and lavender soak in and do what it was supposed to do. I knew that there was a fire in the other room with a big bed, and I wanted to use it. I wanted to feel Damon over me, inside of me, and every way possible, even as I felt myself trying to find a way to sabotage everything.

I felt a little better when the bath was over, rising to dry myself off and drape the robe hanging on the hook on the door over my body. Damon was doing the same, and I walked into the main room to hear the crackle of firewood and see a big, cozy bed. Maybe I was being stupid with my thoughts. This was a wonderful life.

Damon took my hand and led me to the bed slowly. "I don't have a lot of experience in trying to keep a woman around, but I want you to know how much I want to make you happy. I want you to relax, smile, and give yourself to me." He pushed me gently down on the bed and stared into my eyes before he kissed me. Damon pulled my hair down carefully, even as I cringed with the knowledge that it was salty from the ocean air and probably looked awful.

I forgot all of that as he skillfully deepened the kiss, draping himself over me. We moved onto the pillows and made out slowly and sweetly for a long time, and I felt all my doubts slipping away as he pulled the robe away from my body. Damon worshiped me, kissing every inch of my skin as my body heated up for him. His robe was untied and I felt him hard against me as he sucked a nipple into his mouth. "Damon, I need you." His hands slipped down between my legs, finally touching me where I needed it most as I cried out.

Once he was naked and sheathed, Damon plunged inside of me as I gasped. "Let yourself go, Elisa. Don't hold back...not tonight." He drove his cock in deep and slow, and I got lost with the movement. I rocked against him, desperate to come around him as I reached around his body with my hands and legs to pull him closer. "Baby, you feel so good. I don't want to lose you," he murmured, as I felt him harden further inside of me, close to coming.

We both cried out as we came seconds away from one another, and he dropped beside me as I stared into the fire. Nothing would ever feel this good. No man could ever make me feel so complete. I yawned, tired from the day, as he pushed the covers down and we settled under the blankets. "I feel like we should stay up or something," I murmured, fighting the urge to close my eyes.

"Nonsense. We had a big day, and we're both tired. All I need is you here beside me to make me happy." The fire crackled again, and I snuggled close to Damon, feeling his warmth envelop me as I took a slow breath.

I woke up, frightened at first, not knowing where I was. I looked around and felt Damon pressed against me as I stroked his hair and remembered the night before. I looked toward the closed curtain and got out of bed, walking softly across the carpeted floor to pull open the fabric. The ocean was choppy, and I looked at the horizon where the sun was just starting to come up, in colors of pink and orange. My breath caught in my throat as I heard my name across the room.

"Come look. It's beautiful." Damon yawned and walked over to join me, pulling me into his arms as we watched the sky brighten together. "This is amazing."

Damon pulled me back to bed once the sun had risen completely and we kissed under the covers as he ran his hands over my body. "I loved that with you. I want to taste you and feel you again, doze off, and check out at the last possible minute."

"I like that idea," I murmured as he slipped down over my breasts and stomach before ending up between my legs. I learned how incredible an orgasm was first thing in the morning when the room was dim with the morning light. I learned what it felt like to have someone inside of me when I was newly awake and cried out his name both times that Damon made love to me.

We fell asleep, tangled together, for another couple of hours before we made love again. I never wanted to leave this room, since everything was frozen in time here. We didn't have to go to work, or even go back to Boston if we stayed here. I reluctantly showered in the huge tiled space as he joined me, washing my hair carefully so I could do something with it today. I left it down in curls and kept a band around my wrist as I smoothed some moisturizer on my face. I took the clothes from the dresser, pulling them on as I watched Damon dress. He seemed quiet and we looked around the room before we made our way down to the lobby. I helped myself to some coffee while he dealt with the bill before joining me. "Want to eat in the restaurant or find something in town?"

"What's better?" I asked, as I looked out of the windows and let my eyes rest on the ocean waves.

"There's a nice place on the corner. Good food and an amazing view of the water. Sound good?" I nodded as he took my hand and led me to the car, opening the door so I could settle in.

Damon was right. The cafe was small but offered everything he promised, and I added some cream to my coffee as I looked out of the windows. We were both on the quiet side today, eating and wandering around for a bit in town afterward. Damon started back towards the city just after noon, and I leaned back on the comfortable leather seat. I fell asleep as we drove, with the radio playing softly in the background.

We arrived in Boston too soon, and I felt his eyes on me. "Home or my place?"

"I should deal with the roomies," I said slowly, as he beamed at me.

"You're taking the apartment?"

"I am, but we're going to be discussing a rent payment," I warned him, as he headed to my side of town.

"When do you think that you'll be moving in?" Damon asked, as I shrugged. I thought my roommates might be eager to fill the space once I broke the news, though I wasn't sure. He drove to the curb as I looked at the run-down building, already missing everything about the weekend.

"Thank you for everything," I told him, as I turned to look at him. I had paid for our breakfast today, after gave up the fight, but compared to everything he had done, it seemed like nothing to me. "I'll see you tomorrow?"

"It's your day with me. I'll try to keep my hands off you," he promised me, before leaning in for a kiss. Just being in his car was risky, but the brush of his lips against mine could start a lot of rumors.

"See you tomorrow. Thank you," I told him again, as I slipped out of the car with my small bag of belongings. I walked through the complex as I imagined the new place, clean and beautiful.

Mine.

I walked through the door to see the front room empty. I walked back to the tiny shoebox of a bedroom and found Melody studying. "Hi," I greeted her softly as she glanced up with tired eyes. "Where is everyone?"

"You know that I hide in here all of the time. I have no idea. Why?" Melody asked, with curious green eyes.

"I found another apartment. I'll have it all to myself. I wanted to tell everyone together." Melody looked jealous as she pushed a hand through her hair. I could write a check and leave with the few things that I had tonight, running to Damon. I settled for putting my things down and sitting on the bed as I looked around.

"I'm jealous. I'd love to live alone. How did you find it?" Melody asked.

"A friend from work," I told her, as I slipped off the Henley, leaving the thermal on. We talked about school for a bit before I put on my headphones to sleep, covering my eyes. I slipped the jeans off but left the shirt, wishing that it smelled like Damon.

I had an early class, and I got up and put the jeans on with a smile, changing into a sweater from my closet before I headed to the campus. I got coffee and sipped it as I took my seat. I had three classes today before I needed to change for work. I was hoping that I could talk to everyone in the apartment tonight at dinner.

When I came out of my apartment that night, I noticed a familiar car on the curb. Mark smiled at me. "He wanted me to bring you to the office."

"Oh. Thanks." I let him open the door, blushing as I slipped inside and licked my lips. "Is he like this with a lot of people?"

"Damon is selective on who he chooses to help, so I'd say no. I haven't seen him the way that he is with you before, to be honest. I worry that...someone will end up hurt." Mark spoke carefully, as I stared into the front of the car, where he'd left the window down.

"Him or me?"

"Both," Mark replied, as he kept driving towards the office, letting me out at the curb as I told him I'd get out on my own. The car was enough, without the grandiose display of a driver. I smiled at him and walked up the curb in my favorite heels and a simple black skirt and white shirt as I heard someone call my name. I turned my head to see Autumn as she ran over to me with a bag in her hand.

"Nice ride. Do you have a driver or something?" She asked, as I blushed and forced a laugh.

"No, of course not. That's just a friend who saw me leaving and offered a ride. It beats the bus," I laughed, as she nodded and we walked in together.

"How was your weekend?" She asked in a friendly tone, and I realized I could say nothing about it.

"Nothing special. Just hung out around the city," I replied, as she told me about how she had seen a band at a club and loved them. I nodded and smiled at all the right places as we took the elevator upstairs. I decided to hang out with the team for a bit, since I was too nervous to see Damon just yet. We walked in together and Autumn handed out some sandwiches to everybody, offering to split hers with me. "I ate at school, but thank you."

32

DAMON

I glanced at the clock, knowing that Elisa would be arriving soon. I had missed her last night, and I sighed as I heard my cell ring. Glancing at the screen, I saw that it was my attorney, and I answered with a frown. "James. Is everything okay?"

"There are some pictures of you with a woman popping up on some of the gossip sites. Do you want me to prepare something?" He asked as heat flooded my face.

"Fuck. How close are they?" I asked, as I pulled up my computer to do a search. I found them quickly, relieved to see that they were taken at the beach and quite grainy. That was the point when Elisa was all bundled up and wearing her hood as well, so nobody could clearly see her. Of course, the story talked about the inn and my romantic weekend with the mystery woman. I groaned. I didn't understand how we escaped further photos, but I thought I was in the clear. "If anyone asks, it's nothing serious."

"Of course," James agreed, as we ended the call. There had been bits and pieces about me in the gossip columns before and even pictures with women along, with a lot of speculation. That didn't matter before now, since it was never an employee. I didn't want Elisa to suffer the backlash that would come with the publicity. There was a good chance that I'd escape without any damage, but she was just starting her career.

It was a couple of hours later that she tapped on the door and walked inside when I told her it was open. "Good afternoon," Elisa greeted me as she sat down and licked her plum stained lips. She looked stunning in a simple outfit that showed her curves, parts of her that I was very familiar with after this weekend. "How are you?"

"I need to talk to you," I started to say, as her face paled. "There were some pictures this weekend that showed up online. You're not recognizable in them at all, but I wanted you to know in case anyone said anything." All the color drained from her face as I reached out to take her hands.

"Mark drove me in today. You sent him." I nodded, not realizing then what it could do to this situation. "Autumn saw me, and I passed it off as him just being a friend. What if she sees the pictures and someone knows who he is? This wasn't supposed to happen like this, Damon. It has been so brief."

"I have a plan. I will get someone to pose with me in a few convenient places. A friend. That will make everyone think it was her with me at the inn and the beach, and all of this will go away," I told her, as Elisa narrowed her eyes.

"Who?" Her voice was small, and I stroked her hands with my thumb.

"Nobody that I'm involved with, Elisa. She'll only be a prop," I promised her, knowing that I'd slept with Brooke a few times during some drunken nights. She was a friend of the family, and it was never meaningful in the least, but it would get people talking. She just made the most sense in the moment for me. "That is the quickest way to deal with this, before people start digging."

"Fine. Do what you need to." I saw something cross her face before she took a deep breath. "What can I help you with today, assuming we're done with that?"

"I haven't gotten any work done at all today. I've been thinking of you," I told her, as I looked at the door. "Go lock that."

"No. There's enough chance for chatter as it is, Damon. We need to work." I saw her pulling away again as I turned to my computer. I emailed James and told him to make a reservation at a trendy place in town and get Brooke there so we could get that started.

"How did it go last night? Did you tell them?" I asked her. She shook her head. "Why not?"

"We're rarely home at the same time. That's going to be hard, but I was going to try tonight. Should I?" She asked me, as I stared at her silently.

"Of course. The apartment is yours." I cleared my throat. "I can meet you at my place later tonight. I'll send Mark to get you."

"Bad idea. I think that we should just keep our distance for now, so you can...do what it is you're going to do with your prop," Elisa said, as she ran a hand through her hair. "I am going back to the team. We're not going to get anything done today." Elisa stood and walked out, leaving me alone and in shock as I watched her close the door. A part of me wanted to tell her to get back here, and to do everything I could to get her to comply with my wishes as my cock hardened. I couldn't believe that she walked out on me.

I let the urge to demand her return go and focused on the details of tonight. Brooke and I suited each other, at least to the public. She was the wealthy daughter of a CEO and right for me, by society's standards. She was beautiful, but to be honest, the sex was never great and the attraction mild at best. When I got involved with her, I was younger and willing to sleep with anyone who wanted it, and Brooke was convenient. I didn't know how that would affect my plan, but I needed to do something fast.

I stayed in my office, even though I was desperate to talk to Elisa and fix this. I hadn't been in this situation before, but a prop had always calmed down a rumor before. I needed this one fixed immediately.

I made myself go to lunch, just to get some fresh air.

My phone chimed in my pocket, and I found a text from Brooke telling me that she'd meet me, ready to look stunning for the cameras. I rolled my eyes and set the phone down, knowing how much she loved the attention. I kept looking out to the street, and that was when I saw Elisa walking with her team, looking a bit lost. A man was close to her, seeming to guide her, and I narrowed my eyes as he reached for her arm. Elisa looked at him with a slight smile, as if he had caught her off guard, and moved back into the group as they made their way to an Italian restaurant.

I threw the rest of my lunch away and stalked toward the door and back to the office. I was desperate to touch Elisa, and my body raged at me to turn around and claim her, while my remaining logic told me to give her some space. It was useless to try and work, so I just sat at my desk and sipped coffee, only making myself more jittery.

I sent a text to Elisa toward the end of the day, telling her that I missed her. I promised her that everything would be okay, and that we could resume everything, but she only told me to do what I needed to do. I didn't know if she was still moving, working for me, or even what she was doing tonight.

I went home to dress for dinner, since it was one of the best places in the city. Mark picked Brooke up along the way and opened the door, so she could slide into the car. I gave her a glance, seeing that she was dressed in something skimpy before I looked away. "Someone is in a bad mood. What the hell is wrong?" She asked, as she moved closer to me, filling the car with an acrid scent of her floral perfume.

"Nothing. I just need the paps off my ass. You know the drill," I said, as I felt her hands slide over my shoulders and tensed.

"I do, but I also know where this has led us before. I haven't been with a man like you since last time, Damon. Let's have some fun with this." She slipped her hand around my arm and moved closer as I looked outside to see how close we were to the restaurant. This was going to be miserable.

I put on my best smile for the cameras as we left the car, taking Brooke's arm as she beamed. I knew that there was a part of her that got off on this, a part that I was all too familiar with. I was still horny from earlier, and my emotions were all over the place as we walked up the steps and inside, looking every bit the couple that we weren't.

People called out, asking if she was the woman from the beach as Brooke winked coyly at them. With her curly hair recently done in a lighter, caramel shade I figured that someone could easily assume that it was. I kept my head high and my smile charming as I worked the room, feeling Brooke inch closer and closer to me with every step.

We took our seats in a cozy little booth, where she moved close to me yet again and I fought the urge to grit my teeth. "Who is beach girl?" She asked in a whisper, as someone approached to take our drink orders. Brooke ordered a glass of wine and I asked for Hennessey on the rocks as her eyes twinkled. "Did the man with no feelings suddenly develop them? Poor Damon." Her hand slid over my thigh, making me jump.

"You are a prop tonight. Nothing more," I told her in a low voice as the drinks were delivered. I smiled as I thanked the waiter. I assured him that we'd be ready soon as I grabbed the menu, hating my body for reacting to a woman's touch after the day that I had. "Enjoy your free dinner and the spotlight, Brooke. That's all you'll be getting." I gave her a cold look. "You must be lonely after Ben dumped you."

I knew that her engagement had ended recently, one to a good guy who I knew through family connections. I didn't think it would ever happen when I'd heard the news, but Brooke got caught with another man and ended things badly. "That was a bad move. This might boost you up, if you stop acting like a desperate whore."

"Fuck you. You called me, Damon, or had your attorney do it. I think that this night is on your shoulders," she shot back, as the blood in my veins turned to ice. I reminded myself that it was just a few hours. I smiled and faked a toast with her as we read the same menu together. There would be a lot of pictures from this night, and I needed them to be convincing. We stayed at dinner for two hours, and I forced the meal down my throat, smiling and laughing as I flirted with her. We left in the same rush of camera flashes and questions, but I told Mark to pull into my private entrance and let me out before he took Brooke home. She stared at me as I slid toward the door, almost in disbelief. "That's it?"

"I'll see how this works out over the week, and James will contact you if we need a repeat." I got out and closed the door. This was something that we all did from time-to-time, and it wasn't her first rodeo. I didn't understand why she was acting this way, unless she really wanted me to fuck her. I was aching with need, but it was all for Elisa. I watched the car pull back out into the street.

I walked into my empty apartment, feeling the silence heavy in the air. I reached for my phone and saw that there were some Google alerts, but I pulled up the phone screen to call Elisa. The phone that I'd given her was powered off, and I fought the urge to throw my iPhone across the room. I dropped it on the couch and went to take a shower, jerking off like an animal as I played back the times I'd made love to her. I came all over the tile, despondent at the fact that it had been solo, since I'd fucked Elisa in here. I used up all the hot water and dried off, tugging some shorts up my legs before I went back to the living room to do some damage control.

The pictures were surfacing one by one, and I felt sick at how convincing they looked. In an alternate universe, Brooke and I would be a great looking couple, but it wasn't going to be this one. I just hoped that it worked and everything calmed down so I could get Elisa back. I walked into my kitchen for the bottle of whiskey.

The alarm woke me up on the couch as I blinked and looked slowly around. Shit, it was only Tuesday. I needed to be at the office, but I felt like complete shit. In truth, what would I get accomplished? I sent a text to my managers, telling them that I had a bug and was staying home. I could sleep this off and not fight the urge to go find Elisa and beg to talk to her. I stumbled to bed, ignoring the return texts as I left my phone on the couch.

I passed out for a few hours, tossing and turning as I kept waking up from scrambled dreams. I hated the fact that I could still smell Elisa in here, making myself curse the fact that I'd brought her to begin with. I also wondered if I'd ever wash the sheets again as I pulled her pillow to my face and inhaled deeply.

Eventually, I stumbled back to the living room to order some food for delivery and check the gossip sites. Everything was where it should be, and the comical speculation was running rampant. There were murmurs of Brooke and I being back together after her heartbreak from earlier this year and speculation that she was the woman on the beach, off for a romantic weekend with me. I was glad that it seemed to be working, but knew that none of that was true.

There was also a single text from Elisa, asking me if I was okay. She'd heard some mention of my being sick, and I shook my head as I read it. I told her that I missed her, and that I was hungover from that, knowing or hoping that she'd keep these communications to herself. I told her that the previous night was awful. I knew that I was babbling, but I had the sense to stop when there was nothing in return. I didn't want to lose all sense of dignity in this process, so I ate and went back to bed.

The next day, I started the morning with a jog, like I usually did. I was going to make life as normal as possible until this storm settled, hoping that I'd get my prize.

33

ELISA

This whole world was a parody in my eyes. I was in shock when Damon mentioned using a prop to get the rumors deflected. A prop? He was going to dinner with a woman, fake or not. Worse yet, they'd have to act like a couple even more than if they were actually together, for show. I'd heard about these things in Hollywood, never realizing that it applied to business celebrities as well. I got through the work day, assuring my team that I was free to assist them as I laughed along to their jokes and accepted their dinner invitation.

I felt like a fool when I got home and searched for the pictures online. Not only did I find convincing ones from tonight's dinner, but a few other occasions where Damon had dated this woman. Her name was Brooke, and she was tall and gorgeous, exuding sexuality with every movement. There was no way that they'd never slept together.

I also found the pictures that he'd mentioned to me, and they were grainy and distant. I didn't even recognize myself in those, but there was one in town with my back to the camera that seemed like it looked more like me. Apparently, the paparazzi in smaller cities were less aggressive than Boston.

Conveniently, Brooke had a hair texture like mine and a hair color that could be easily mistaken for me. Did this woman do that this day for her role? I didn't understand any of it as I pored over the pictures of them at dinner. Damon was laughing, holding her hand as they walked in and out of the restaurant, toasting her with a warm smile on his face, and, the worst one of all, the kiss outside, before they got into the car. Fake or not, it was long and intense, and it made all the food in my stomach want to rise right back up.

Still, when I heard that he was out sick, I couldn't help but send him a text. No matter how I was feeling, I wanted him to be happy. I hated myself for offering the olive branch and shut the effort down when he responded to me later.

I still hadn't mentioned the apartment to my roommates, despite thinking about it every moment. It wasn't just for my perks, but for my mother. She'd have a better place to live, and, at this point, I'd live with her and find a way to pay some rent. That was what mattered to me the most, and I'd suffer through the job, internship, and a hundred other ones to take care of my mom.

When Melody asked what was going on, I told her that things might have changed and went back to studying in my small bed. "That's good. I like sharing this space with you, even if it is the size of a closet." I smiled at her and told her the same, wondering if there might be a friendship forming there.

Wednesday was my day to work with Damon, but I had weighed that heavily in my mind during my sleepless night. I could intern, go to school, and work a part time job to afford the apartment. It would be crazy, but tons of college students did that every day. It wasn't permanent, and I would graduate sooner rather than later and get a great job. I did get some financial aid, but it wasn't a great deal, and not enough to support my mother and me.

I decided to talk to Brent and tell him that I was just going to be sticking with the internship. I'd blame school and family issues, which usually worked and were the truth. I would compose an email to Damon and send it off, feeling motivated by the offer of a weekend job at the coffee shop in my favorite bookstore. I could keep my financial aid with the few hours and hopefully budget enough in for some-thing for Mom and me.

I did the email from my laptop, surprised that the weak Wi-Fi was working so well. It sounded professional, and I thought that I sounded upset as I explained a phantom college issue, asking to be replaced. I offered all the items that he gave me for the new person, as well as any passwords that he'd given me. I didn't want anything to do with the job anymore, and I hit send before leaving for my classes that day.

I changed into a dress at the apartment and took a bus to work. I had the phone, along with everything else, in my bag, powered down. I intended to work with my team today. I'd made myself clear in the email. I stepped onto the elevator, finding it empty for a change as I glanced around and pushed the button for my floor. Surprisingly, the elevator stopped on Damon's floor, and I stared forward into his icy blue eyes before he told me to meet him in his office and walked away.

It was obvious that he'd received the email, that he was, at the very least, angry, and that I'd be in for it once I reached his office. I licked my glossed lips and walked out calmly, as if I was just going in for my shift. Nobody seemed to notice me as I approached his door and tapped softly, my stomach in knots. Damon was standing at his desk, staring at me as emotions crossed his face, one after the other.

"What the fuck was that email about?" He asked, as I stood in a stunned silence, not knowing what to say. "Do you want to pretend that you never knew me, when I've been thinking about you every fucking second of every single day, Elisa? Do you want to pretend that we mean nothing to each other?"

"Damon, I..." He walked over to me, his hands capturing my face as I started to talk again. "No, don't do this." Even saying that, I made no effort to pull away. I was intoxicated by his heat and his scent, feeling dizzy in his presence. I reached forward, clutching his shirt as I closed my eyes and dropped my head forward. "I want to be over you."

"No, you don't." His lips captured mine as he lifted my face to his, claiming me. I felt my lips part as his tongue met mine, dancing in my mouth. I felt my arms slide around his neck as he lifted me and carried me somewhere. I didn't care where, since I was consumed with my want for him.

Damon made quick work of lifting my dress when I was on the couch, opening my bra as he sucked a nipple into his mouth. "Oh, God," I murmured, as his teeth dragged against me.

"I want to take you home and tie you up, Elisa. I want to fuck you for hours after you put me through this." He pulled away and stared at me. "I did all of that this week to protect you from the media. It worked. They think that I'm with Brooke now, after one dinner, and everyone has all but forgotten the pictures over the weekend. My ploy worked, but I know that it hurt you and I feel horrible inside."

"I know what you did, Damon. I am just so confused about your world." He pressed his lips to mine softly before pulling away again.

"I am sometimes too." He slipped my panties down, spreading my legs as he took on my glistening pussy. I was turned on and needy for him as he slipped a finger through my folds. "Nothing happened that night. We went, and I came home alone right after. Everything in those pictures was staged, Elisa." I jerked as he found my clit and stroked it.

"You kissed her," I murmured, as he continued his slow torture. "She wanted you, Damon. I could see it in her eyes."

"She wants her fifteen minutes of fame, any way that she can get it. I'm just a pawn in her game," he responded as a finger slid inside of me. I arched my back and reached my hands over my head to grip the cushions as I closed my eyes. "That was the most pre-meditated fake kiss that I've ever given, and it made me sick. It made me want you."

He added a finger, and I rocked against him, weak and greedy for my release. I was torn between control or just letting go when I felt his mouth over me, sucking me between his teeth. "So close," I whispered, sliding one hand into his hair as I continued to hold tight with the other. Damon licked and sucked at me, bringing me close before I exploded before him. Oh, fuck...it felt like it had been months since I'd been with him, when it was only days, and the orgasm pulsed through my body as he kept tasting me. "I need you to fuck me," I told him, as I stared into his eyes.

I climbed onto my knees willingly as he dropped his pants, spreading my legs for him as I heard a wrapper being torn. "I want nothing more," Damon promised me, as he took me with a hard, deep thrust. He gripped my ass tightly with his hand, making me cry out as he kept thrusting. I was wet and tight around him, just where I needed to be, as our bodies slapped together. "So fucking tight. So meant for me." I rocked with him, my dress off and somewhere on the couch. "Come for me, Elisa. I need to feel you again." I pushed back as my legs trembled, weak as I orgasmed with him.

We collapsed together on the leather and I closed my eyes. All my progress was gone now and I wondered what to do.

"Why the email?" Damon asked.

"I wanted to avoid you and keep the internship. I can get a part time job, and, along with my financial aid, I think that I can take care of Mom and me," I replied, as he shook his head at me.

"You text me out of concern when you're probably pissed off at me, and you worry about your mother. What did I do to deserve a woman like you?" Damon asked, as I honestly shrugged. "I was talking to a colleague earlier today after I got that email."

"Not this again. I want to do this on my own," I groaned, as he placed a finger over my lips, one that tasted like me.

"It isn't what you think. It is the sister company to this one, equal in success. He is looking for an assistant to help with the growing industry. He asked about my new staff, and I told him about you, as my employee. I forwarded your resume to him, and he looked it over, saying he was quite impressed. He is ready to offer you a full-time job, at the same wage that I was paying you, Elisa. It's still in the city and close by, and you could do everything you want to with it."

"He doesn't know that I'm involved with you?" I asked, and Damon shook his head. "He really liked what he read?" Damon nodded.

"He even contacted Brent and asked him a few questions, getting stellar feedback. This is real," Damon told me.

"I need to think about it," I told him. He frowned. "This is huge, and I appreciate all of it, but I need time. Can I have his info, and I'll call him tomorrow?" Damon told nodded, and I leaned in for a kiss. "Does anyone else know about the email I sent you?"

"No," he said softly, sadness crossing his face. "It's hard to believe that you won't be in here with me, no matter what happens in your career. It's worth it to have a chance with you, though. That's all I want," Damon said, as he pulled me down for another kiss.

"Do you still want to tie me up and fuck me for hours in your house?" I asked, as he slipped his tongue between my lips.

"More than anything."

"Good," I replied, as I moved over him, needing his warmth. "I'll come over tonight, and we can discuss every detail of this offer over dinner before you show me how much you care about me." I smiled. "I need the opinion of a professional after I make a call later today."

Damon looked down between us where my slick folds were sliding over his hard cock. "You say that sitting like this on me."

"Are you clean?" I asked, as a bold thought crossed my mind.

"I get checked regularly and always use condoms," Damon confirmed, as I looked down. I had been on the birth control shot for years now, just out of habit, and just in case I met the right guy in college. His eyes were dark and hungry as I dragged my lip between my teeth and raised myself, letting him stand tall. "Elisa...fuck, I want you bare."

I leaned down to kiss him as my body wrapped around him, nothing between us. The sensations were incredible, and I moaned against his mouth as he reached forward to hold my hips. Damon guided me slowly, telling me that I felt so good that he wanted to explode, in between long kisses.

We made love there, slow and sweet. I felt his heat deep inside as he came for me, sliding my panties back on to hold it before I dropped down beside him again.

34

DAMON

Elisa cleaned up and went to join her team, promising me that she'd be over at six to spend the evening with me. I returned to my desk, shaking my head as I played back the hours I'd just spent with her. I thought she was quitting and leaving me when I got that email full of excuses as to why she could no longer work for me. I thought that she was denying everything that I offered to her. The pain was incredible, and I stared at the security screens until I saw her walk in, intending to demand her to stay.

Burt had called in that time, inquiring about my interns. He was a good man and ran the same company as I did, a branch of this one that was just a tad smaller. Kenneth needed another building to handle his overflowing client list and Mark and James became his new baby, though he handed it off to a different staff of people. I spoke to them frequently when I took over, but not on this level. I was looking for a way to compromise with Elisa's standards, while staying with her and I brought her up, offering to forward her resume.

Burt was impressed and told me that he wanted to speak to a few others that worked closely with Elisa, since I claimed I didn't know her too well. I agreed, giving him a couple of numbers before I hung up.

That had calmed me down, and I stood when I saw Elisa approaching the bank of elevators. Somehow, she stepped into an empty one and I went to meet it, pushing the button to make it stop. I knew where all the elevators went in the building, having learned those details when I updated the security in the building after we fired a troublesome intern. It was after that when I considered ditching the intern program altogether, but I was talked out of it.

Now, I was relieved that I'd kept it going, since it brought me Elisa.

I thought about the possibilities as I left a bit early, wanting to get some errands done before she arrived. I bought something to make for dinner, while I had Mark go get some roses at the best florist in the city. Together, we brought everything into my house, as he told me how much Brooke had sulked on the way to her condo. I laughed when he said that she met up with a guy outside and left with him a few minutes later.

I explained that, with any luck, I wouldn't have to pull a stunt like that again. I wanted Elisa and nobody else. I felt the need to shrink back from the public eye so much and just settle into as normal of a life as I could find. Even if it wasn't with Elisa, I needed to go in that direction. This was exhausting.

I set the roses up on the counter and loaded the food into my fridge. I was planning to make some salmon, fresh vegetables, and salad, as well as serve eclairs from a great bakery beside the grocery store for dessert. I felt good about the job offer and hoped that Elisa would as well, given that it was everything that she'd been working towards. She needed to see past the way that she got it and focus on the fact that she'd earned it.

I glanced at the clock and realized that I had an hour before Elisa would arrive and went to take a shower. I gripped myself under the hot water, unable to get the memory of her riding me today out of my head. I hadn't felt the heat of a girl against me since I was teenager, before I'd gotten smart about protection. Jerking off, I cried out her name as I shot against the tile again, breathing deeply.

I dressed in jeans and a blue Henley, leaving my feet bare. I headed down into the kitchen and read some of my favorite salmon recipes, deciding on a simple dish, with some butter drizzled over the fish. .

I wandered the apartment, even though my maid had been there that morning. I had her pop in every couple of weeks to make sure things were clean, even with my regular picking up. Growing up with a mother who depended on help had ruined me for life, and I'd never go back. I lit some candles and made a fire before I heard the knock at the door. Wetting my lips, I walked over to the front door.

"Hi," Elisa said, with a beautiful smile, as I looked her up and down. She was wearing the jeans I had bought her, which clung to her curves perfectly, and she'd paired it with a long-sleeved cashmere sweater that highlighted her full breasts. "Is casual okay?"

"You look downright edible," I told her, as I held the door open and reached for her hand. Elisa laughed as she came inside and looked around with an impressed gaze. "Like it?"

"Are you trying to woo me, Damon?" Elisa asked, as I kissed her softly while closing the door.

"Is it working?" I asked, before I claimed her lips again, reaching down to cup her ass as I drew her closer to me. "I'm going to make some dinner, too. I have good wine. I might even let you get to second base, if you're lucky."

"Mmmm, that has promise," she remarked, as she wrapped her arms around my neck. I laughed and led her to the kitchen where she watched me prepare the fish for the oven. Elisa offered to chop the vegetables for me and sauté them in olive oil with some seasonings and garlic. She was a natural in a kitchen, and we chatted about light subjects as we got the food ready, finishing the salad together. I poured some wine, and we sat at the small table together to drink it and talk. "I called Burt today."

"How did that go?"

"He's very genuine, and I think he sounds professional. He admitted that he's taking a chance with an intern, but with my schooling and resume, he's willing to take that chance," Elisa replied, as I nodded. All of that was legitimate, and I'd considered it all before deciding to hire her for myself. "I would start at a slightly lower wage, until I passed probation, but Burt assured me that you'd be willing to take me back, should anything happen. I seem to be well liked at Elkus Manfredi."

"You are, and I would, apart from the fact that we'll be dating if you take that job. That might pose a problem."

"I even asked Brent about it, and he said to go for it," she said, as I smiled. "I am going to. I am going to try and not be stubborn about it because of your involvement."

I pulled her close to me for a hug as I stood up, and she held me tightly. "Does that mean that you'll forgive me?" I asked.

"I know why you did that now," Elisa admitted, as she smiled ruefully. "It drew attention away from the weekend, even though I was jealous and must have looked at those pictures a hundred time the following morning. I analyzed them, but when I see you look at me, I know that you don't have feelings for her. There was no sincerity in your eyes. I also found it funny when she had pictures the same night at a club, drunk with another guy, while the headlines speculated that you'd had a horrible fight. You need to choose a better prop, Damon. She's amateur."

"I don't want a prop. I want a girlfriend," I told her. "I want a woman to spoil and make love to all over my house. I want a woman to cook for and pamper. I want a woman to support as she moves up the ladder in my industry."

"Taking any applications?" Elisa teased, as she pressed closer to me, kissing me hungrily.

"There's only one woman for me," I assured her, kissing her eagerly as we made our way to the couch. I had her shirt off, and I was sucking on her sweet nipple when the oven beeped and we both groaned. "Damn it."

We both stumbled in, and I pulled out the fish just in time, while she turned on the stove to give the veggies a quick reheat. Elisa had already cooked them, but had left them covered to soak in their flavors and stay warm. I plated the fish, and she heaped her side dish on the plates before we both finished with some fresh salad. We took them back to the table, eating as she asked me what to expect across the street.

"What about the apartment?" I asked, as we washed the dishes together.

"Well, it's for employees of Elkus Manfredi, so I want to save it for them. I have been doing some looking of my own and found a cute place near here that my mom and I could share. I'll be able to afford it with the new salary, even losing the financial aid. I just hope that I don't get fired."

"You won't. You'll be a graduate before you know it and have the world at your fingertips," I teased her, as Elisa laughed and kissed me again. Her eyes grew dark as she gazed at me and I felt the heat in the room. Elisa took my hand and led me across the room to the door that hadn't been opened since last time she was over. I grabbed a key from my pocket, unlocking it, and pushing it open as she walked boldly inside.

"I loved the dinner. I loved the roses. I loved everything about tonight, but right now…I want you to fuck me." I hardened at her request, so direct and bold, as I closed the door and dropped the key on a counter. "I want what we couldn't do in the office, Damon." I told her to take my pants down before she dropped to her knees, searching my face. I nodded, and she leaned in to take my cock in her mouth. I held onto her hair, loose and wild around her shoulders, as I rocked my hips with her movements. Her hand gripped my ass, digging into my skin, and pulling me forward as I buried myself down her throat. Her moans joined my cries as we moved harder and rougher, her name passing through my lips as I filled her. She felt so good and drank me down as I stared down at her. "Elisa," I said, with wonder in my eyes as I pulled back and offered her my hand.

I handcuffed her to the headboard with metal covered by soft cloth, after I stripped her. I left the black lace thong on for the time being, obsessed with the scrap of material that separated me from what I wanted more than anything right now. I left her legs free as I moved down her body, biting and nipping my way over her neck and nipples as she arched her back for me.

I knew she wanted it rough as she begged me for more as I moved down her stomach. I found a small but powerful dildo and slipped it inside of her, securing it with the lace as I kept her legs open for access to her clit. I ravaged her as the device vibrated, giving me more and more sweet honey as she came closer to a release.

"Damon!" Elisa cried out, her face flushed with desire as she clenched her fists. "Oh, fuck. I'm coming." I dragged her clit between my lips as she screamed through her peak before I pulled the panties off and slid the dildo out of her body.

"So intense." I moved her to her stomach, careful with the restraints as she moaned. I knew that she was already tired, but I was nowhere near finished. I spread her legs and smacked her ass, watching her jerk in front of me as she begged for more.

Elisa screamed for me to fuck her after a few smacks, and I slid inside, once again bare. I gripped her ass and squeezed as I took her repeatedly, knowing that her moans were of pleasure, not pain. I pulled back and drove myself inside one more time before I filled her, feeling her tight, wet pussy wrap around me. I cried out her name as I held her hips tightly and memorized the feeling of her body.

Elisa surprised me by asking about what other toys I had. I showed them to her, describing what they would do to her as her eyes heated up. There were several dildos, some plugs, and a variety of things to use for spanking.

Elisa asked if I could use them in my bedroom, and I picked up her favorites and brought them with us. "I love that room, and the possibilities that come with it, but I want to make this our place as well. I want to experiment in here and then fall asleep in your arms," she confessed as she blushed. I lit a few candles in there, and we dropped on the mattress, still bare.

"You are the first woman that I've been with here, in this room." I waved my hand around as I spoke, and she looked at me with bright eyes. "This is the last place I see at night and the first thing in the morning. I don't want to invite anything in to the one place I find peace. I want you here, though."

"I want to be here. I want to try, but it's going to have its hard moments. There will be tough times." She looked at me. "I know about your past, and I've read the rumors. It's difficult to think about, but I do see the way that you look at me, so I'm willing to give it a chance."

"Good," I said, as I kissed her and watched her move onto the mattress, lying on her back. "So, what do you want to try first?"

35

ELISA

I had always thought that sex was boring. I thought that it was never like it was in movies or books, but with Damon it was better than any of that. I read a lot of romance books, thanks to having a million roommates, and they got pretty hot. It was unbelievable. This somehow seemed like it could be real and work out, though I didn't have a lot to base that on. I hadn't spent a lot of time with Damon, but what little time we had spent together had been memorable. I fell asleep that night knowing a lot more about sex toys than I'd ever imagined, but happy in Damon's arms as I held onto the hope that I had for us.

The following day at work, Brent made the announcement that I was moving across the street for a full-time position. The team was happy for me, though I sensed a bit of confused jealousy. Still, they took me to lunch to celebrate, and we clinked our soda glasses together as Autumn asked how it came to be.

"Burt called asking about the interns, and Brent recommended me. He sent over my resume and it impressed Burt, so he asked me if I'd like to work for him. I guess it's not totally out of the ordinary for someone graduating in a year, right?" I asked, as I dipped a fry into some of the ranch dressing on my plate.

"That's when I got hired," Vince admitted with a grin.

"Me, too," Autumn said, as she smiled. "They're willing to give us a chance when they see that we've worked hard. A lot of the time, they don't want to pull long-time staff, since we work in teams. It's nice." She sipped her soda. "Is the big boss upset that he's losing your help?"

"No, I was told he gave me a good referral. He told me good luck," I responded, with a bright smile on my face. I could never reveal the truth, and what might end up out there would be decided after I left the building. It would be something that developed later, and I hoped that's how it would be perceived.

"He seems busy with that floozy these days. I don't know what Damon sees in Brooke, apart from their family ties. I mean, I know they hooked up a few times, but to keep going back? She was caught with another guy at the club the same night the pictures were taken." Autumn shook her head and I frowned. He had said they weren't involved like that. "Whatever. He's gorgeous, but seems a bit dumb to me."

"I don't know him well," I lied, as the conversation moved to something else. Gossip about Damon seemed like it got boring fast, and I wondered about the truth about us. Would I be the floozy then? We finished our lunch, and I thanked everyone before we headed back to the office.

Damon was walking with Brent to the elevators ahead of us. He looked good in fitted black slacks and a blue shirt, hidden under his black winter coat. I stared at him as everyone chatted around me, losing myself in the memories of last night.

Someone called his name across the lobby and Damon turned around, his brows furrowed together. He said something to Brent and waited as a woman with familiar hair walked up to him.

Brooke.

Damon looked annoyed as he talked to her, but I managed to sneak by unseen. She was pretty in person, and she was busy grabbing his arms and shoulders as they talked. I wasn't lying when I told him that this was going to be difficult. He had a lot of past, whereas I had next to nothing. I made my way back to our room, looking around wistfully for a moment. "What's up?" Vince asked, as he set his cup down on the floor.

"I think I'm going to miss this place. I was barely here, but you are such a good team to work with," I replied, as he smiled.

"You're going to be the assistant to the big boss. That's something to look forward to." Vince assured me.

"It's scary," I whispered, as we gathered around the table. "I'll be full time and going to school. The hours will be crazy, and I might drop dead from exhaustion."

"I hope your guy won't mind that," Vince said.

"I am building an empire. He needs to understand that." I smiled, and he nodded as Autumn smirked at me. I knew from talking to her that Autumn grounded herself with the company before she had said yes to her fiancé's proposal, and they were now planning the wedding. She was a go-getter like I was, coming from a poor family that had struggled as well.

I was going to be with the team for another two weeks before I started across the street. I jotted down advice that everyone gave me, since the job would be a little different. I knew that Burt wanted me to learn various duties, and I hoped that some of it was hands-on design. That's what I loved, after all.

I saw Damon every night that I could, but didn't have the guts to ask him what Brooke wanted that day. I felt uncertain all over again, and, when we were in one of the beds in his house, he noticed it. "What's wrong?"

"Nothing. Just nervous," I replied, with a smile on my face. I hadn't gotten high fives from everyone in the building, and found that Devin was a little jealous of my job offer. That made me worry that Damon had influenced the process more than he was telling me, making me wonder how much of this life was earned. I wanted it all to be mine.

"You have this in the bag, Elisa. Just go shine." He dropped the toy he'd been using on the night stand and looked me over, seeing that I was flushed and tired from the torment that he'd just put me through. "Is someone bugging you at the office?"

"No. They're just not all thrilled for me," I admitted, as he gave me a dark look. "I'm sure it's normal, and I just have a few days left, right?" I wouldn't see Damon daily, then, and would have so much more to wonder about.

"Sure. You'll settle in before you know it and be telling me all kinds of stories." Damon teased, his eyes warm on me as my heart jumped into my throat. "We'll be rivals."

"Hardly," I choked, as I dropped onto the pillow and took a deep breath. "I have years to go for that."

"You doubt yourself too much," Damon reminded me, as he moved beside me and traced my stomach with his finger. "You'll get this job, and we'll only get better and better."

"I hope so." I closed my eyes and let my body relax as sleep took me over. As uncertain as I might be about Damon at times, my body craved him, and I knew that I'd never get enough. This made me tired. "We're exclusive, right?" The idea that we were having unprotected sex a lot lingered in my mind every time we were finished. Not that I had any worry about pregnancy, because the shot was virtually a sure thing, but I worried that he was sleeping with other women.

"Did you ever think that we weren't?" He asked, as I felt him kiss my hair.

"Just curious." He turned the light off and pulled me against him as he kissed my cheek.

"You know you're it for me."

The holidays were coming, and my new office was decorated in style as I walked through the doors to meet with Burt and fill out paperwork. The staff had thrown me a party on Friday, and I had lingered with the friends I'd made, while Damon stood on the other side of the room with his managers. We shared a few glances, but kept it to a minimum with so many people around. The food was excellent and the cake beautiful, with a champagne toast in my honor. A few of the people were going to a bar afterward, and they invited me. I glanced over at Damon. "Come on. There's cause to celebrate."

"Okay. Sounds great," I agreed as she smiled and pulled out her phone to send a text. Within an hour, things were wrapping up, and I thanked everyone for making it great there as I held my glass up high again. I left with my former team and a few others, walking to a group of bars on the corner. They were getting busy with the after-work crowd, and we blended into the crowd at the bar at the first one.

I had a feeling to look at the door, and I saw Damon walking in with the other guys. I frowned for a moment as I turned back and accepted the round of drinks that Vince bought everybody and thanked him as we clinked our glasses together. I knew that I would keep in touch with Vince and Autumn, and I stood closest to them as she waved across the bar.

"This is Tim, my fiancé!" I looked at the tall, dark-haired man and shook his hand as she introduced all of us. They looked good together, matching one another's style, and he introduced a couple of friends who had come along with him.

Dave was one and Glen the other, and they had the same alternative look that Tim did. Glen congratulated me on the promotion once he heard about it, and drew me aside to start talking about my new job. I felt eyes on me and glanced over to see Damon staring at me angrily before someone walked up to him. Brooke again. Ploy, my ass. I smiled at Glen and focused on his words, pretending that I wasn't crazy about the man across the bar with another woman.

The drinks were flowing, and I kept downing them as they were offered, laughing a little too hard at Glenn's jokes. I even danced with him, crazy and free as reality left my mind, and I lived in a different world. It wasn't until I had to pee that it hit me like a sound punch in the stomach. I did my business and walked out to feel someone grab my arm and pull me down to the end of the dark hallway.

"What the hell?" I asked, as I looked up to see Damon dragging me. "What are you doing? Isn't your date missing you?"

"Date?" He asked, as he reached the end and stared down at me.

"Brooke. I've seen you with her a few times, and I give up," I yelled, as he grasped my shoulders to stop me from flailing my arms.

"A few times?" He asked, and I nodded as I took a deep breath.

"At work, here...and there's all those pictures of you with her. I know that you hooked up in the past, too." His face fell as he stared at me, and all my happy buzz turned into hard, painful emotions. "I've been with you all this time, wondering who else you're with, as I'm taking chance after chance. I must be stupid."

"Who the fuck told you that?" Damon asked, as I stared sadly at him.

"Is it true?" His silence told me everything. "I wish it was you. Now it looks like you were hiding something from me, and I keep seeing her. I don't even know what I want anymore."

"I was a mess that day. Everything happened with the pictures from the weekend, and I knew I had to hide who you were. She was the first thought, and I didn't want you to be worried about things, because nothing has happened between Brooke and I for years." Damon insisted. "She is here by chance tonight, and she wanted to tell me something about my parents in the building that day. That's it, Elisa." His eyes darkened. "How do you explain the new guy? You look like you're having a great time with him. Who is he?"

"I don't know!" I told him, as I tugged my arm away from him. I hurried through the bar and out into the streets, crying as I searched my purse for my phone to get a ride home. I had the job that I always dreamed of, but at a cost I never expected. I was in love with Damon, but too insecure and jealous to trust in him. I saw a cab and held my hand up as I ran towards it. The last thing I saw before we drove away was Damon staring at me, and I turned forward and told the driver where I lived.

I was alone that night, and I huddled under my covers, crying. I had given him back all the devices, and my phone was shut off. I wouldn't be hearing from him, and I hoped that he didn't come over. I needed some space.

36

DAMON

I watched Elisa drive away in the cab in shock. She was drunk, but hadn't made any sense in there. I took a breath of the fresh, cold air before I turned and walked back into the bar. Brooke had been here by chance, and she was with her friends now. For that matter, she was dating a new guy, and didn't even seem concerned with what I was doing. The other time had been a business call, though I'd had no idea that Elisa saw us. I wish that she would've brought it up, so we could talk about it before it blew up like this.

I cast a dark look at the man that she had been dancing with, before I sat down at the table with my friends, sipping my fresh beer. He seemed to be looking around for her, and I couldn't blame him.

I knew that she was gone if she didn't try to reach out to me. I knew where her apartment was, but I was going to try to resist being a caveman and dragging her out of it and back to my place where she belonged. Fuck, I wanted to ask her to move in with me, and we'd set her mom up somewhere close by, tonight of all times. I didn't see any reason to hide our relationship, now that she had her new job.

I drank myself into oblivion before calling Mark for a ride home. I called Elisa several times in the car, getting her voice mail every time. "Damn it."

"What's wrong?" Mark asked, as he glanced at me in the mirror.

"The past is coming back to haunt me, Mark. I didn't tell her everything that I should have, and it's the one thing I got in trouble with."

"Can you fix it?" Mark asked, as I frowned.

"Maybe. I can get roses again and have them delivered. I could try to get her to talk to me." I wasn't sure what to do. This was all new to me. I was supposed to be going home with her after the celebration over her promotion. It was nice to see her smiling and so happy about the catered work party, looking beautiful in a paisley wrap dress and black heels. I was going to ask her to move in in front of the fire in my room, when I told her how much I loved her.

Now, that was gone.

"I tried to save my marriage before things went south. I took her to the coast, got a great hotel, and took her to dinner. It worked for a while, but we were too far gone. Arrange a weekend away."

That reminded me of our trip before, and I considered the idea. We could stay a couple of nights and make a longer trip of it.

"I don't think you're that bad off, since you've been seeing so much of her. I just think you fucked up a bit. I learned that communication was everything when I got divorced, and I'd advise you to learn from it."

"Yeah. I see your point," I told him, as he pulled up to the curb. I got out and went upstairs, feeling drunk and empty as I took off my clothes and fell into bed.

I called Mom and Kenneth the following morning, arranging to meet them for dinner that night since they were home. We met at a steakhouse and I sat across from them as Kenneth watched Mom get her jacket off with a warm gaze. "How are things at the office?" Kenneth asked, once we had our drinks in front of us and orders were placed.

"Going well. There are a few new clients, and the earnings are coming in." Kenneth still got a good chunk of that, and he nodded with a pleased expression.

"Did you get any good interns this round?" Mom asked, as my face fell. "Damon?"

"Yeah, we did. One of them just got hired full-time by Burt." Damon sipped his whiskey and nodded. "She's great."

"She's moving up fast. What is her position there?" Kenneth asked, as mom searched my face with a knowing gaze.

"His assistant. She was with Brent's team and helped me a bit here and there as well," I replied, as I took a long sip of my own whiskey. "She's graduating from MIT in a year."

"I think she sounds like the perfect addition for Burt. You guys always get the cream of the crop with the annual internship program." We ate as our entrees came, and mom pressed the napkin to her lips as Kenneth excused himself to use the bathroom.

"When did you realize that you'd fallen for her?" Her eyes sparkled at me, exact copies of mine.

"Recently, when I messed up. I was trying to fight it, but, Mom, she's addicting. Compassionate, beautiful, intelligent, and she's stubborn as a damn mule. She wants the world." I shrugged and looked at her.

"Isn't that better than the empty women who only wanted you for your money?" Mom asked. "Speaking of which, I'd be thrilled if you stopped doing photo ops with Brooke. I adore her parents, but she's not the woman I want as a daughter-in-law."

"Not even close. I was dodging some rumors," I told her, as she giggled.

"The woman on the beach? I saw those. That was the intern?"

"It was."

Kenneth returned, and sat down, glancing between us.

"What's your mother worried about now?"

"Damon found a woman," she said, as I scowled. "He fell for one of the interns."

"I dated her while she worked there. I didn't intend for that to happen, but it did. I thought when she moved across the street, we could start fresh. She just...I think she thinks my past is too much."

They both laughed. "It is," Mom said, as Kenneth kissed her hair.

"If I got over all the trouble this man got into, there's hope for you. Woo her. Show her what a great man you are."

I went home that night thinking about what she said. I knew that I was in love with Elisa, and that there was nobody else for me. I needed to tell her that. I asked Mark for some advice as we drove, smiling at his romantic ideas.

I did some work on my plan over the weekend, setting up reservations for the following weekend at the same place we had stayed in Cape Cod. I asked for the most romantic room they had and a lot of additions to get my plan in motion. I made a couple of reservations at good places, leaving time to do what we wanted on a whim.

The rest could wait until I was going to surprise Elisa, and I dropped into bed, staring at the ceiling as I hoped that it worked.

Work wasn't the same without Elisa there. I missed her being in my office with her beautiful smile and laugh, and I stared at her number on my phone. I wasn't going to call her yet.

37

ELISA

The new office was merely a smaller version of Elkus Manfredi, but it was still new to me. I reported to duty with Burt, wearing a new black pencil skirt, a white shirt, and the shoes that would always remind me of Damon.

I missed him more than I wanted to admit, but I was drunk and foolish at the bar that night. I'd made an excuse that I drank too much to Vince and Autumn and left because I felt sick, since only Damon saw me run out and jump into the cab like the chicken that I was.

Burt was kind and gave me the same devices as Damon, showing me the way he did things with patience and kindness. He remarked at how quickly I picked things up a few times, and I always credited Damon and Brent. Burt was surprised that I'd worked so closely with Damon, since it wasn't mentioned over the phone. "Really?" I asked, as I looked at him.

"All Damon did was say that you seemed to be doing well and sent me your resume. It was Brent's recommendation that got me, and your school record. That's impressive, with your grades and skills," Burt assured me.

I felt a little bad as I left that night, tired and emotionally drained.

I went and showered, pulling on my pajamas, and going right to bed. Damon didn't set me up with my job, like I'd thought. He threw my name out there, but I earned it with my hard work, and I sighed. I picked up my phone, making sure that my alarms were set, and found his number. I considered calling him, but my mind was mush. I needed to figure out what to say.

It was suddenly Thursday, and I was ready for the weekend. I sat at my desk at lunch and stared at my phone again, then looked across the street to Damon's building. The more time that passed, the sillier it seemed to make the call. I put my phone down and tore my sandwich into pieces as I berated myself for getting so drunk that night. I'd had lunch with Vince and Autumn yesterday, and they went on about their new project, making me miss that part of my internship. I knew that I'd be doing it soon, but for now, Burt was training me on assistant duties. I went back to my office with a forced smile and confidence for my future, staring blankly at my phone as I thought about Damon. I didn't dare ask them about him, because I didn't want to blow his cover.

I left the office on Thursday, glum, and looking forward to the weekend. I glanced up as someone handed me a rose, confused. Another person did the same thing, a stranger that I didn't know. What was going on? I stepped forward, receiving a few more until I saw Damon holding a big bouquet in his arms. "What are you doing?"

"I am trying to woo you," he replied, as I smiled. "Is it working?"

"It's creative. I liked getting these," I told him, holding up the loose roses. "I've been wanting to call you. I didn't. I felt like an idiot for that night."

"I know what I did wrong. It made sense to hide that at the time, but looking back, I know it was a mistake." He looked in my face, searching for something. "I missed you. I was hoping that we could have dinner tonight and discuss something."

I looked around. It didn't matter if we were seen, because we didn't work together. There would be rumors, but they didn't matter. I just wanted to know Damon and everything that scared me about

him. I wanted to make an informed decision about love, now that I
was laying the groundwork for the rest of my life. "Yes, I'd like that.
Where would you like to go?"

He took my hand, still holding my flowers in his arm. A few
people looked at us with smiles as we walked to an Italian place a few
blocks away. Once we were seated, we stared at each other until the
waitress brought our wine.

He held his glass up once it was there. "To us." I clinked it and
smiled as he looked into my eyes.

"I am sorry that I flew off the handle, Damon. I should have just
asked about her, like I should have asked about a lot of things."

Over dinner, we talked about the women in his past. He explained
that he'd had wild times and made some mistakes, but that was over
now. He knew that he wanted to be with me. I told him that I felt the
same, and we fell silent for a moment.

"I want to take you back to the coast tomorrow night. I have a
reservation for two nights, and we can really explore the area" He
told me when we left the restaurant. "I need to get out of the city."

"I think that I do as well." He asked me to come over and I agreed.
We walked together, and he asked me about the job. I told him that it
was confusing and that I still felt lost, even though Burt told me that I
was doing well. Damon assured me that I was. All new jobs started
out that way, but I'd settle in and feel like I was home. That was
another reason that he planned the trip for me, and I smiled as he
unlocked his door.

I walked into more roses and gasped as I looked around. "I figured
you didn't have a new place yet, so I thought that we'd keep them
here." Damon looked at me. "How is that going?"

"I stayed when things fell through. I knew that you would let me
have that apartment, but I figured I'd find something of my own after
the new year." I smiled. "My roomie, Melody, might go in on something with me. She hates it there as well." His face seemed to fall, and
I stared at him. "What? She's nice. I promise."

"I just want some alone time with you. That's all." He pouted, and
I stepped closer to him, taking a deep breath. Words couldn't describe

how much I had missed Damon, but I hoped my eyes did as I gazed into his face. I cupped his face and smiled as I pushed up on my toes.

"You'll have a lot, no matter what." I brushed my lips against his slowly as he inhaled, sliding his hands over my waist. "You consume me." I kissed him in between sentences. "I can't stop thinking about you." Another kiss. "I don't want to be without you." I gave him a last gentle kiss. "I don't want to worry about stupid shit." The next kiss was hungry, and he pulled me closer as he deepened the kiss eagerly.

"Is it bad to have sex before we go away?" He asked, as I giggled and wrapped my legs around him.

"No, it's perfect. I can't wait," I told him, as he carried me up the stairs to his bedroom. I didn't ask why we weren't in the other room. He stripped me roughly and kissed me hard. He kissed every inch of my body slowly, edging me closer to a release before he'd pull away. I begged him to take me in a hoarse voice, as frustration filled me, finally weeping when he settled between my legs and sucked on my pussy.

"This pussy is mine. Do you hear that?" He asked me, before drawing my clit between his lips.

"Yes, it's yours." I agreed, gripping the sheets as he ravaged me. I came hard when he had spent enough time on my clit, crying out his name as I rocked against him.

"I haven't thought about another woman since we met. I've been obsessed with you." He told me, as he rose and settled between my thighs. "I want you, Elisa."

"I want you," I replied, as he lifted his hips and positioned himself before driving himself inside of me. I moaned as he filled me, sliding against my walls. I pulled him closer as he kissed my neck, sucking the skin between his teeth, as he moved just a little harder and faster.

We came together, and I arched my back, feeling him bite down on my nipple. "Oh, oh, oh." I gave in to my feelings for him, holding them in until sometime this weekend when it felt right to say.

I stayed the night, waking up early so that Mark could take me home to change. I threw on a dress after a quick shower, making myself look decent. I didn't have time to pack, because Damon had distracted me all night in bed, but I'd figure it out tonight. It was only two nights.

I drifted through the day with a smile, a little dazed as I tried to focus on my work. I was picking it up fine, but I had a lot on my mind and stole several looks across the street. Damon had been perfect last night, making me feel like the only woman in the world from the moment that I saw him. We met for lunch, enjoying a sandwich together as we discussed the trip and held hands. I kissed him on the street, not caring who saw. I had my life falling right into place before my eyes.

I hurried home to pack, taking just a few minutes before I called Damon to tell him that I was ready. He promised me that he'd see me in a few minutes, and I zipped up my bag and glanced around the tiny room.

"Have fun." Melody smiled at me from her bed. She'd started seeing someone from school, and it seemed to be getting serious. They were going to a concert the following day and getting a hotel.

"You too. Check out Jared for me!" I winked as I grabbed my stuff and walked out of the apartment to meet Damon. The drive was great, and we laughed the entire way, stopping for a quick dinner at one of the diners near the inn, before we checked in for the night.

The room was better than last time. It was bigger, with a spa in the bathroom instead of the ,and a generous balcony overlooking the ocean. However, it was also colder. "We'll come back when we can actually wear shorts one time," Damon promised me, as I smiled at the view.

"It's fine. This is lovely," I assured him, as I looked into his eyes. We went back into the room and got into the spa for a bit before finding a movie in bed. I snuggled against him and looked around with a happy sigh. "Thank you. I needed this, and I needed you with it."

38

DAMON

I watched her sleep after we made love, with a beautiful, peaceful look on her face. She was wild tonight, initiating everything as she rolled me over to my back. I was going to pop the surprise on her after that, but we were both tired. We had two days here, with nowhere to be but a couple of restaurants. It was going to be perfect.

I woke up to see the sky dimly lit through the balcony doors, and shook Elisa gently awake, so we could watch the sunrise. She photographed every step of it with her camera, trying different angles as I watched her. "We'll be sure to watch it go down from a beach as well." I told her, as she nodded.

When the sun was up, and we were cold, Elisa dragged me back to bed and kissed me as she pressed her body against me, knowing that her hard nipples would be hard for me to resist.

We made love carelessly before dozing off again in the beautiful room, waking up hungry, and in need of coffee. We both showered quickly and headed down to the in-house bistro, ordering their special with coffee as we stared over the expansive ocean. It was warm enough to walk around, and we took advantage of that, finding new beaches and more shops. I could tell the Elisa was in love with the town, making me fall more in love with her.

We went to a nice place for dinner and watched the sunset before going back to our room. She wanted to use the spa again, resting her body against me as she sighed. "Thank you. Today was perfect."

"I wanted to ask you something, Elisa." I said, as she tensed before me. "I did a lot of thinking in this crazy time since we've been seeing each other. I've changed, and it was confusing, but a learning experience."

"Agreed," she giggled, as her hands slid up my legs.

"I knew something in the beginning, but I had to mull it over. I think I needed space to say this, but ... I love you." I felt her freeze as her nails dug into my skin.

"Love?"

"Yes. I love you completely, and I want to make things right with us. There's something else."

"Oh, God." Her voice was almost a whisper, and I kissed her hair.

"Not that fast," I promised her as I took a deep breath. "I am going to be buying an apartment complex as an investment very soon to spread some money around. It's nice, close to work, and safer than that POS you live in now." Elisa opened her mouth to speak, and I covered her mouth gently. "I can offer you something in there, as well as your mom, but I'd like you to move in with me."

I heard her start to cry. "I love you, too. I hated being without you." She wiped at her eyes, and I pulled her close. "I want to live with you, because we've spent too much time apart."

"Give notice when we get back, and get your ass in my place, then." I teased her, as I kissed her neck. "Let's do this, Elisa."

We stayed in the hot water as long as we could stand it, before drying off and going to bed. I left only one light on by the bed as I kissed her, happier than I've ever been. "There's one more thing. I want you and your mother to have Thanksgiving with my family. Will you?"

"I'm meeting your parents?" Elisa squealed, as I kissed her again.

We made love, her on her stomach, her ass in the air as I took her hard. I'd given her one orgasm with my mouth already, and she was tight and wet for me. We woke up to do that several times before watching the sunrise again, wrapped in robes. Elisa suggested an early morning walk on the beach to look for shells, and I agreed.

She found a lot of shells and rocks, dropping them into a bag that she'd brought along. Everything was quiet, and it felt like we were the only people on Earth. "This is great, isn't it?"

"Yes. It's such a change from the city, which I love too...but I'll miss this."

"Maybe we'll get a house here, down the line. Come up every weekend and just chill. It can be big enough for family." She pressed against me for long kiss. "I love you."

"I love you." We held hands as we wandered back to the car, looking over the scenery as we glanced down for more shells.

We headed home that afternoon, and Elisa moved in with her few things by the middle of the week. She paid the roommates a month ahead of rent, so they wouldn't get in a bind, and I took her to dinner the first night that she was officially living with me.

Someone heard about us at work, but I assured them that we had held off on dating until she left the company. Once a couple of weeks passed, it seemed to die down and many people liked me being settled down. They said I was less grumpy and a nicer boss, particularly Brent and the other managers.

THE END

ABOUT THE AUTHOR

Mrs. Love writes about smart, sexy women and the hot alpha billionaires who love them. She has found her own happily ever after with her dream husband and adorable 6 and 2 year old kids. Currently, Michelle is hard at work on the next book in the series, and trying to stay off the Internet.

"Thank you for supporting an indie author. Anything you can do, whether it be writing a review, or even simply telling a fellow reader that you enjoyed this. Thanks

🌸 Created with Vellum

CPSIA information can be obtained
at www.ICGtesting.com
Printed in the USA
BVHW011921151121
621714BV00002B/15